BREAK-IN & EGGS

A BLUE HAVEN COZY MYSTERY

C.G. FOUTZ

Copyright © 2021 by Courtney G. Foutz

Break-In & Eggs

All rights reserved, including the right to reproduce this book or portions thereof in any form whatsoever except in the case of brief quotations embodied in critical articles and reviews.

Break-In & Eggs is a work of fiction. Any references to historical events, real people or real places are a product of the author's imagination and used fictitiously. Any resemblance to actual persons (living or dead), events, or locations is entirely coincidental.

Dedication

To my sweet husband for loving the sandy beaches of North Carolina as much as I do and joining in on all the adventures that fill my soul.

CHAPTER ONE

Deep Dish Isn't Just for Pizza

Whether it's a quiche, an omelet, or a soufflé, don't walk—run to the Savory Egg Cafe. From your very first bite you'll know why owner and chef Wanda Hemmings has yet to be defeated at the Quiche on the Beach Bake Off. The texture, taste, and seasoning of every menu item is unmatched. The deep dish spinach and bacon quiche is my favorite, but I've also heard chatter that the mushroom and goat cheese quiche is another top contender. Wanda's special ingredient is written at the bottom of every menu. She says local eggs from Farmer Don are the key to why everything tastes so fresh and delicious. I bet that makes Farmer Don blush. Go taste the difference for yourself, and be sure to come back here and let me know what you think!

Love ya lattes,
Von Reklaw

***

"Alright Scout, the blog is finished!"

I hit the button on my keyboard that would send my latest blog post to the front and center of my website. My golden-haired companion, who was curled up on his bed next to my desk, jumped up as soon as he heard the click of the laptop closing. As always, I stumbled out of my office trying not to trip over Scout. He was five years young and still hadn't figured out personal space.

Even with the number of times I'd almost dove headfirst onto the floor after tripping over him, I was still thankful to have him by my side as I settled into our new town.

The coat rack at the front of the house where Scout's leash hung was one of the many things I'd chosen not to upgrade when I'd moved in. I remembered my grandmother hanging my coat there each night after I'd come in from playing in the yard. Now I used it more for Scout than for myself, but I still loved thinking of my grandmother every time I reached for his leash.

"Come here, boy!" I patted my thighs and braced myself as Scout came running. The entry hall of the farmhouse I now called home was covered with the original hardwood flooring and Scout hadn't quite figured it out yet. Once he got close, he'd try to stop and all seventy pounds of him would coast right into me.

I slid the collar around his neck, clipped on the leash, and patted his head one more time before opening the door to the fresh, humid air of a July morning. It was barely nine o'clock, but the heat was already in full force. I thought that all of my family visits to Blue Haven, North Carolina during the hot August summers would have prepared me for what the South called hot, but I was wrong. Living in it day in and day out is much different than a vacation.

I'd only been living in Blue Haven for six months, and two months in I had learned to surrender any attempt to straighten my hair before I left the house in the morning. An hour's worth of pulling a straightener through my hair was defeated within ten minutes of walking out my door. So, this morning, when Scout and I headed out, my hair was pinned on the top of my head and a baggy tank top covered the waistband on my mesh leggings.

"Good morning, Veronica!" I turned my head to find Mr. Gordon waving at me from his driveway.

"Hi, Mr. Gordon," I said. "Off for your morning stroll?"

"You betcha. At my age, I've got to move all I can," he smiled. "How about you? Out to walk the dogs today?"

"We sure are. GiGi is waiting for us," I said.

Mr. Gordon let out a scowl. Poor GiGi. It wasn't fair that a five-pound Yorkie was judged by the actions of her owner, but when your owner is Wanda Hemmings, it was hard not to be. The same Wanda Hemmings who had won the annual Quiche on the Beach Bake Off for the past decade. If the town had the voting power, that probably wouldn't have been the case. I guess that's why they'd brought in a panel of culinary professionals for an unbiased opinion.

I had tried to like Wanda when I'd first moved to town, but her nose-in-the-air, too-good-for-this-town attitude had made it really hard. Her cafe was popular with tourists though. There was always a line outside the Savory Egg Cafe for Sunday brunch. She was a great cook, and she made sure that everyone knew it. I tolerated her more than the rest of the town because she was a great customer. Her long hours running the cafe on the boardwalk meant someone had to walk her dog.

"You be careful now," Mr. Gordon yelled as he turned opposite of me from his driveway. "That woman is a witch, I swear."

"Will do, Mr. Gordon. You have a good walk." I waved one last time before Scout and I headed to the fork at the end of the street. One right turn and a stroll past half a dozen oak trees and we'd be walking up the steps of Wanda's front porch.

I'd first walked up those steps with my dog walking business flyer about two weeks after I'd moved into my grandmother's farmhouse. I'd been still in shock. My life in New York City had been torn apart and I'd had no idea what I was going to do in Blue Haven, but it was her final wish that when her time came, I would take on the farmhouse. So, I'd packed up Scout and whatever I could fit into the back of my car from my bedroom in a shared apartment on the Upper East side, left my cheating, Broadway-dancing boyfriend behind, and driven ten hours south until I'd pulled past the blue welcome sign into Blue Haven. It had been a familiar feel. I'd done it many times before.

I had grown up loving Blue Haven. Every summer my parents and I had made the road trip down from the suburbs of New York to visit my grandmother and help with the upkeep of the farmhouse. My grandfather had passed away before I was born and the five-bedroom house had been a lot for my grandmother to handle on her own, especially as she grew older. This was the only home she'd ever owned and with all my grandfather's memories in it, she'd refused my father's suggestion of selling it for something smaller. She'd been determined to keep it in the family.

Scout pulled me down the brick walkway that led to Wanda's front porch. His leash slipped out of my grasp and I juggled it between my hands before it hit the ground. I yelled Scout's name and luckily, he froze long enough for me to regain control. I heard a chuckle and looked over to see that Betty Jean had stopped pulling weeds from her garden to watch my and Scout's antics.

"That dog always ends up walking *you*, doesn't he?" Betty Jean yelled.

"He sure does," I said. "Your garden is looking good, Betty Jean. You have quite the green thumb. That's something I did not inherit from my grandmother. I'm having the hardest time keeping her garden alive."

"Thank you, dear! Why don't you stop over sometime? Those purple ones over there—" Betty Jean pointed to the side of her white-trimmed porch. "Those are azaleas. They're just like the ones in your grandmother's front yard. I can show you how to care for them."

"I will take you up on that! Thanks, Betty Jean."

She nodded, wiped the sweat from her forehead and dug her garden rake back into the dirt. One thing I loved about Blue Haven was the willingness of people to help me fit in. My grandmother had been a well-liked member of the town and the need to make sure that her granddaughter was taken care of was top of the minds of people like Betty Jean.

I watched her dig a few more weeds out of the dirt before the sound of GiGi's bark from inside Wanda's house reminded me what I was there for. Like most of the town, Wanda never locked her door. I heard GiGi's nails tapping on the other side of it and when I turned the knob and opened the door, I saw her dark, wet nose peeking through.

"Hey, sweet thing," I said. Scout pranced in behind me and both he and GiGi began a wrestling match on the pink-and-white-striped aisle runner while I went to grab GiGi's leash. This had become such a familiar routine that I didn't even look back at the sound of their snarls.

"Okay, you two. That's enough of that. It's time for coffee."

I hooked GiGi's pink leash on her diamond-studded collar and untangled the two furry beasts long enough to get them out the door and back onto the gravel road that would lead us down to Lattes All Day, my favorite coffee shop right smack dab in the middle of the hustle and bustle of this small beach town.

CHAPTER TWO

I could feel some of the wooden planks moving under my feet as I strolled down the boardwalk, Scout and GiGi pulling me past the open shops. The crowd was out in droves for that early on a weekday morning. The sound of the ocean waves was covered by the tropical music that played through the speakers of the souvenir shop, and surf boards were propped up against the window of Sal's Surf Shack, which was the oldest store in this town. Sal was proud of it. I waved at him as I walked past and found my way to the line of Lattes All Day.

Many of the cafes along the boardwalk served coffee on their menu, but the two-decades-old inflatable pink flamingo, holding a coffee cup and wearing a pair of black sunglasses over his eyes, always drew in the crowd here at Lattes All Day. It was the perfect photo opportunity for tourists, who were constantly making their way in and out of Blue Haven.

I watched as strangers smiled next to Pinky the Flamingo. That wasn't officially his name, but it was the secret name I'd given him back when I could barely see over the coffee counter. That line moved a little slower than the one in front of me. I didn't even realize I'd made it to the front until I heard a familiar voice.

"Good morning, Veronica!"

I turned my head to see Abigail standing on the other side of the coffee window. Abigail was the owner's daughter. She was a teenager, working the morning shift on the weekends. Her blonde hair was tied back tightly into a bun, and she snapped her bubblegum while typing my order into the register.

"Hey Abigail!" I waved. "One medium vanilla latte, please."

"Coming right up, Veronica! That'll be four dollars and eighty-two pennies."

I reached down into the side pocket of my yoga pants where I always stuffed my credit card, but it was empty. Shoot! I'd been so focused on getting the blog published that I had completely forgotten to grab my card off the kitchen counter before heading out that morning.

"Abigail, I'm so sorry! I forgot my credit card and didn't even realize it."

"That's okay," Abigail said. "You know the drill. I'll put it on your tab. Come back and pay it when you can."

A sigh of relief escaped from between my lips. Sadly, this was something I had done before. Many times. An honor system like this is not something that would fly back in New York City. As a matter of fact, it seemed like something I'd be writing articles about at my old job as a crime blotter writer. I could see the headline: "Perp gets roasted after stiffing coffee shop." But in a town like Blue Haven, you're given the benefit of the doubt here at Lattes All Day. If you're a resident and can't pay, you get added to the tab and pay later. I'd always paid my tab, but forgetting my credit card, well, it'd become a regular thing at that point.

"Thanks, Abigail. You're the best!"

She gave me a nod and slid my latte through the window. I took in the strong aroma of espresso and pressed the cup to my lips. It was pure heaven on an early Sunday morning, but it didn't last long. Scout had noticed a seagull swoop down in front of him. I felt the pull on my arm. I tried to stand my ground, but Scout was too strong. Suddenly my body was lunging forward and headed straight for the pile of crumbs the seagull was attempting to snatch.

"Scout!" I yelled, holding onto my latte and the leashes for dear life. GiGi jumped in as we got closer to the seagull. Unlike Scout's deep bark, GiGi's was high-pitched and burned through my ears. I stumbled behind them for a few feet until I finally caught my balance. Then I pulled on Scout's leash and turned my bad dog voice on. "Scout, no!" I yelled. He immediately came to a halt and sunk himself onto the ground. "That's what I thought," I said, feeling somewhat accomplished even with all the eyes that were staring at me.

My bad dog voice didn't scare GiGi, though. She had taken over for Scout and was frantically trying to break free of my grasp in order to catch the seagull. I was so focused on trying to get her to calm down that I hadn't realized Wanda had snuck up behind me until she called out.

"GiGi, what is Mama's girl doing over here?" I turned around to see Wanda kneeling in front of me. She clapped her hands together and immediately caught GiGi's attention. Before I could blink, GiGi had jumped into Wanda's arms and was bathing her wrinkled cheeks with wet, slobbery kisses.

"I'm so sorry, Wanda," I said. "I didn't mean to cause a commotion." Wanda's cafe was only two stores down from Lattes All Day and just so happened to be less than ten feet from the pile of crumbs the poor seagull had never gotten the chance to enjoy.

"Now I see why my GiGi has taken up so many new antics at home. That boy of yours is a bad influence." Wanda waved her finger at Scout.

I took a deep breath and smiled. My hand was gripping Scout's leash so tight that I could feel my fingernails digging into my palms. If anyone was a bad influence, it was GiGi. Her non-stop barking at everyone that walked by us has made Scout more vocal since our move to Blue Haven. Was I really trying to justify the actions of my dog right now? I shook my head. I wasn't going to let Wanda get to me.

"I'm sorry, Wanda," I said. "It won't happen again."

"Let's hope not," she said, handing GiGi back over to me. "I'd hate to take my business elsewhere." Wanda gave GiGi one last pat on the head before I started back down the boardwalk with my blood boiling. "Oh, Veronica." I turned quickly to see Wanda waving. "Stop by here tomorrow morning. I'll be in early for deliveries. Maybe around 7:30. I'll have your check."

"Sounds great, Wanda. I'll see you then."

It was about time. If I were like Lattes All Day and started a tab for all the money Wanda owed me for my dog walking services, it would be a mile long. Wanda shared custody of GiGi with her ex-husband Jerry. I was unable to escape the stories she would tell about how he refused to put money toward the dog walking when he was perfectly capable of watching the dog himself. Wanda, being as stubborn as the town knew her to be, did not allow Jerry to have GiGi on days that weren't his. That's where I came in.

Wanda's argument was that if she and Jerry were still together, she wouldn't need a dog walker, but since he'd decided to stray from their marriage, he should be responsible for payment. It had taken a couple of months, but Jerry had finally given in, on an *I'll get you the money when I get it to you* basis. That meant I never got paid on time. Every week I'd heard, "I'll leave your check on the counter," but of course, when I showed up, there was no check. Weekly pay turned into monthly payments with Wanda.

I couldn't afford to lose her business. My food blog was just starting to pick up, but it would be a while before I could monetize it enough to make a living. Besides, being a dog walker had its perks when it came to being the mystery food critic in town.

I could be everywhere I needed to be and no one would know I was there doing research. They thought I was sitting enjoying breakfast, or a coffee, while letting the dogs get a chance to bask in the sunshine. And, thankfully, with a clever pen name thought up by my best friend Gemma in New York City, I'd been able to keep my identity a secret.

I shook off Wanda's words. GiGi was wiggling so that I could barely keep a grasp on her with one arm. I bent down and set her back on the ground next to Scout. I didn't realize as I was scolding the two of them for their behavior that someone had walked up behind me.

"I don't know how you deal with that woman on a regular basis."

I looked up to find Suzy Atwater staring down at me. Her hands were pressed firmly on her hips. Suzy was Wanda's biggest rival on the strip. They battled back and forth regularly during peak tourist season over which of their brunch places was more popular. I personally thought it was hard to choose. Wanda's Savory Egg Cafe had killer quiches, but Suzy's Peaches Cafe offered waffles that were to die for. Their rivalry didn't stop on the strip of Blue Haven's boardwalk; Suzy and Wanda had been battling for first place at the Quiche on the Beach Bake Off for years. Suzy had yet to pull herself out of the runner's-up seat. This year, though, she was swearing she had the quiche recipe that would knock Wanda off the top of the podium.

"Hey, Ms. Suzy," I said.

"Wanda Hemmings is positively awful," Suzy said.

"That seems to be the consensus around here," I laughed. "She has her good moments, though."

"Ha! If she does, I haven't seen them in the thirty-plus years I've known her. You're an angel, dear, for putting up with her."

Suzy never called anyone by their name. She called everyone 'dear.' I smiled when I heard it because my grandmother used to do the same. I saw more similarities between Suzy and my grandmother the more I got to know her. Her curly hair and thick-framed glasses were almost a spitting image of the way my grandmother had worn both.

Scout was starting to get antsy from being in one place for such a long time. He gripped his teeth around his leash and I felt the pull between my fingers. I looked down at him wide-eyed, but in his stubbornness, he wasn't backing down.

"It was good to see you, Ms. Suzy, but I think this guy still has some energy to burn off. Have a good day," I said.

"You too, dear."

I nodded and then Scout, GiGi and I walked quickly from the boardwalk and down the gravel road back to Wanda's house. Once I'd settled GiGi back in, Scout and I went on to the next house of the day. We continued on until the evening set in and I could go back to my real job. I organized all the pieces I wanted to write and spent the rest of the night typing away until my eyes were too heavy to stay awake.

CHAPTER THREE

Lavender Lattes Are So Yesterday

I have heard the newest latte at Lattes All Day is an absolute delight! People have been using words like "Heavenly," "Out of this world," and "Addictive." Who knew that rose in a latte would be such a hit? It's so popular that Lattes All Day sold out within hours of the launch. Don't worry though—they're stocked up now. You'll no longer have your heart broken if you show up after the morning rush.

I recommend adding a splash of honey or vanilla to your next rose latte. It gives the floral notes the perfect hint of sweetness. All rose lattes are decorated with a small floral decoration on top. It's great for a photo opportunity, but I don't recommend eating it.

If you haven't tried the rose latte yet, make a note for your next trip to Lattes All Day and tell them that Von Reklaw sent you!

Love ya lattes,
Von Reklaw

***

Another day, another dollar in the dog walking world for me. The rose latte from Lattes All Day I'd written about recently sounded amazing as I rolled out of bed a little after six. The room was still foggy as I brushed my teeth and slipped out of my pajamas and into something relatively presentable to head next door. It was too early for Scout. He never woke up before the sun. I left him curled up at the bottom of my bed while I headed out. My neighbor, Beth, was a night shift nurse, and when her boyfriend couldn't help, I was happy to take her Saint Bernard for a walk. Jefferson was one hundred and forty pounds of pure love. Before I could even call his name, he was in the entry hallway slithering on his back, waiting for me to pet his belly.

"You're such a big teddy bear, Jefferson," I said, bending down beside him.

A few minutes of belly rubs later and he was ready to hit the pavement. I slipped his brown leather harness around him and clipped him in. Jefferson hobbled down the sidewalk and we made it to the road just in time to see Mr. Gordon drive by. I waved and figured he was probably coming back from the morning water aerobics class where he liked to start his week.

Jefferson was the total opposite of Scout. He didn't need mile-long walks to curb his energy. He did his thing as quickly as possible and then pulled me back to the door. I let him in, scooped some food into his bowl, and patted his oversized head while he lay on his bed in the living room.

"I'll see you later, bud!" I said, before slipping my shoes back on and heading out the door.

I looked at my watch. It was almost seven. The sun had pushed its way through the clouds. Scout was surely awake by now. I wanted to get him outside quickly before I headed to Wanda's. Taking him with me the day after she'd accosted him for his behavior probably wasn't the best idea.

Scout was wagging his long, furry tail behind the wooden front door of the farmhouse. I could see him through the frosted glass. Unlike the rest of the town, I locked my door. I'd grown up in the suburbs right outside of New

York City and no matter how hard people here in Blue Haven tried to convince me, there was no way I trusted anyone that much. I pulled the keys from my purse, slipped them into the lock, and opened the door for Scout to run out. He took off running laps around the perimeter of the property. A few times his feet fell out from under him and he slid into parts of the white picket fence that locked him in.

"Okay Scout, come here boy!" I yelled from the swing of the wrap-around porch. "I've got to get going."

To my surprise, he came on the first call, barreled past me, and slid right down the hallway's wood floor into the blue clay vase my parents had given me as a housewarming gift. There was no way I was getting there in time to catch it. All I could do was throw my hands over my mouth, close my eyes and wait for the crash. It never came. The vase steadied itself, thank goodness. I shook my head and let out a loud sigh. I loved my little accident-prone mutt. He stood up onto his all fours and I blew him a kiss, promised him I wouldn't be gone long, and locked the door again.

***

The boardwalk wasn't quite awake yet when I arrived. Most places didn't open until 8 am. This was the beach after all. Anyone up early was either surfing the waves or running on the beach before the crowd got there. They wouldn't be grabbing their coffee or sitting down for a bite to eat until afterwards.

I saw the white delivery van parked down at the end of the boardwalk outside of Peaches Cafe. Two men were wheeling in a tall stack of cardboard boxes, but it was desolate at Wanda's cafe. I walked up and thought it was slightly off that the front door was propped open. She had mentioned that she too had deliveries this morning, so I assumed they'd forgotten to close it, or maybe they hadn't arrived yet and Wanda had left it open, ready for them. The lights were on and there was the faint sound of music coming from the kitchen. A mixture of lavender and sage filled the air.

"Hello?" I said once I'd stepped past the first set of pink and white tables. "Wanda, it's Veronica." I walked in further. "I'm here to pick up my check."

Still no answer. When I got up to the counter, I saw an envelope with my name on it. I grabbed it and peeked inside. There was a check with the amount owed. I yelled out for Wanda again. No answer. I drummed my fingers onto the marble countertop and looked up at the second hand ticking around the clock on the wall. It was three minutes after the time I was supposed to be here. Yet the only sound in the room was a crackling that turned my gaze.

"The stove's on?" I whispered. That was strange. Right next to the flame of the gas stove was an open carton of a dozen eggs. I yelled out for Wanda one more time. I didn't want to leave the cafe empty with the stove on, so when I was still met with no answer, I decided I'd turn the stove off myself. I tucked the envelope into my purse and walked around to the other side of the counter where I would discover that Wanda had been here the entire time.

A blood-curdling scream escaped me as I jumped back. Behind the counter, lying on the white tile floor, was Wanda. She was motionless. Next to her head was an upside-down frying pan. I tried to scream again, but my lungs felt like they were filled with water. Nothing came out. I fell against the wall and that's when I saw the blood. It had come from a gash on the side of her head.

I'd written about all sorts of petty crimes at my job in New York City, but never about anything like this. Was it a robbery? An accident? I had no idea. I slid myself down the wall and wrapped my hands around my knees while I whispered Wanda's name again.

"Wanda? Wanda?" There was still no movement.

My purse slid off my shoulder and when it hit the floor my phone flew out. The screen lit up with a photo of Scout and the time. It was seven thirty-five. That's the time I realized my scream had carried much further than the inside of the cafe walls. I looked up to find a group of people racing through the door. One of them was Mae, the owner of Scented Wicks, the candle shop across the way. She lived in the apartment above her store. I didn't recognize the other two faces.

"What happened honey? Are you okay?" Mae ran over to me. I couldn't move a single muscle in my body to try and stop her. When she passed the counter she too saw Wanda in the small pool of blood and screamed.

"Call 911!" Mae shouted to the men standing in the doorway.

"Do you think she's... dead?" I gulped out the last word.

Mae crawled over slowly. It took her a few times to draw up the courage to place her fingers on Wanda's neck. The color of her skin drained and she turned to me, paler than a ghost.

"I think so."

I'd seen a lot of things during my time in New York City. However, I'd never thought the first time I would see a dead body would be here, in a boardwalk cafe, in the small, quiet town of Blue Haven. And as I had been the first one here, finding Wanda like that, I had to wonder, when the police arrived, if all fingers would point to me.

CHAPTER FOUR

I never knew back when I wrote my very first blog post about Wanda's cafe that one day I'd be sitting here, on the floor with my back pressed against the wall, waiting for the police to arrive. I couldn't take my eyes off the dried dark-red pool weaved throughout Wanda's gray hair, even when a shadow covered me.

"Ma'am... ma'am, are you okay?" There was a deep voice coming from above me.

"Of course she's not okay! The poor woman saw a dead body before her morning coffee."

I looked up to find Mae standing next to a stocky, bald man in a police uniform. He was staring down with a concerned look in his dark eyes. Mae bent down to help me stand. My entire body was shaking so much that even as I came to my feet, I still needed the weight of the wall and Mae's arms to keep me upright.

"Ma'am, I'm Detective Richard Hart. Can you tell me your name?"

I folded my hands over my chest to try and hide the goosebumps that somehow were able to survive in seventy-degree weather. My name? Was that the first question they asked someone they considered a suspect? I swallowed hard trying to clear the ball-sized lump that was now stuck in my throat.

"Veronica," I said. "Veronica Walker."

He scribbled my name down on his notepad. "What's your relationship with the victim?"

"I... I'm her... dog walker. I came to pick up my paycheck."

I reached down into my purse to search for the envelope. It's about that time that a well-dressed man and woman walked through the still-open door. The woman had her chestnut brown hair pulled back into a low ponytail that fell midway down her white button-up shirt. Her eyes were weathered as if she'd been up for days. She immediately walked over to Wanda's body.

The man, dressed in khaki pants and a navy polo shirt, walked over to me. The blue of his eyes helped to pull me from the scene I was currently standing in. They were light, like the clear sky painted outside the cafe window. A pair of sunglasses rested on top of his sandy brown hair.

"Well, isn't this something," he said once he was standing next to Detective Hart.

"Twenty-two years on the force here in Blue Haven and this is my first dead body," said Detective Hart. He turned his head and raised his hand in my direction. "This is the lady who found her: Veronica Walker." I waved like I'd won some kind of prize.

"Veronica Walker," the man with the blue eyes repeated. He reached out his hand and I met him halfway. "I don't believe we've met. I'm Special Agent Declan Grant, one of only two crime scene investigators in this county. I just started last week. They told me it'd be an easy gig. That this town was quiet and uneventful."

I was still mesmerized by Special Agent Declan Grant's eyes, even though the paleness of my reflection was mortifying. I tried not to make it obvious when I slid my hand over my hair to tame the pieces that had fallen from my ponytail.

"Can you tell us anything else about what you saw this morning?" the agent asked.

"Well... special agent," I started. He quickly interrupted.

"Declan is fine."

"Oh, okay—Declan. Well, Wanda told me to stop by this morning to pick up the check she owed me for walking her dog, GiGi. I got here about seven-thirty. The front door was propped open. I walked in, called out for Wanda, but no one answered. When I got to the counter, I saw this envelope with my name on it and noticed that the burner on the stove was on. I didn't want to leave with the open flame on, so I walked around the counter to turn it off and that's when I saw Wanda."

Declan was scribbling furiously into his notepad. His lips pursed together as he concentrated on every word I said. The click of a camera pulled my glance over to the woman who was still crouched over Wanda's body.

"Was there anything else out of place that you can think of?" Declan asked.

"Not that I know of. Wanda had said she had deliveries coming this morning, so I figured that was why the door was propped open," I said.

"And you," Declan turned to Mae, "what's your relationship with the victim?"

Mae rubbed her fingers to her chin. "We're neighbors, I suppose. I own the candle shop across the street and live above it. I just finished putting these heat curlers in. I was still in my nightgown when I heard an awful sound from outside my window and ran down." Mae patted the oversized curlers that were still in her box-dyed, toffee-colored hair. "When I got down to the street, I saw that man run in here, so I followed and saw poor Veronica all shaken up."

"Can you two think of anyone who might want to harm Ms. Hemmings?" Declan asked.

Mae and I looked at each other. The list was quickly growing in my head, and by Mae's wide eyes I could tell her mind was doing the same. Declan's question should have been, "Can you think of anyone in this town who didn't want to harm Wanda?" That list was surely shorter.

"Do you know Wanda?" I asked Declan.

"Not really, but I've heard plenty in my short time here," he responded. "As an agent on this case, I need to remain neutral."

Before Mae or I could provide any possible suspects, the woman who had walked in with Declan came over to us. Her camera was secured on her chest by a strap around her neck. Her straight-lipped smile evaporated all humor from our conversation.

"Ladies, this is Special Agent Parks."

The woman nodded in acknowledgment but didn't take her eyes off Declan. I could tell by her stiff shoulders that she was all business. That made sense, considering we were standing in the midst of a murder investigation and there was a dead body less than five feet from us. I shuddered again at that thought.

"Victim is sixty-two years old. This is a very odd scene. To be honest, all signs point to an accident. There's a blood spatter on the counter and the cash register, but none on the cast iron frying pan next to her. At first glance, it looks like the victim was getting ready to start cooking. There was a recipe card in her back pocket. She slipped while holding the frying pan, hit her head on the counter, and then again when she fell to the floor. There's only one thing that makes me think otherwise."

"What's that?" Declan asked.

"Her shirt. The bottom of the sleeve is ripped and there was a button found on the opposite side of the kitchen that matches the one she's missing on her collar. That screams altercation to me. I really do think we have a murder on our hands."

A murder right here in Blue Haven—I still couldn't wrap my head around it. Gossip was always the front runner of this town, but I'd never imagined anyone to be capable of such a thing.

"Time of death?" Declan asked.

"I'd say about half-past six."

Declan looked over at me. "I hate to ask this, but do you have anyone that can corroborate your story for today? That you arrived here when you said you did?"

"I had to walk my neighbor's dog this morning. I got there around six-thirty. I played with him for a few minutes and then we went for a walk. Mr. Gordon saw me. We waved at each other. And I have security cameras that would have me on there," I said.

Declan scribbled more words on his notepad, but I felt pretty confident that my alibi would check out. Even if I were guilty, which obviously I wasn't, there was no way Mr. Gordon would throw me under the bus. His feelings for Wanda would make sure of it. That's when my mouth dropped.

It had been only shortly after six-thirty when I'd seen Mr. Gordon returning home. Maybe he hadn't been at his water aerobics class. Maybe he'd been coming home from killing Wanda! But what motive would he have? What motive would anyone have? Mae may have had the answer. She leaned closer to me. I could feel the velcro from her curlers pressing into my scalp.

"My money is on Jerry. Isn't the ex-husband always the usual suspect?" Mae asked.

Wanda was recently divorced. She'd never spoken highly of her ex-husband. I'd heard her on the phone a couple of times with Jerry and most of the conversation had involved her berating him. I wouldn't blame him if he'd had enough, but I had inside information. I knew it wasn't possible for Jerry to have killed Wanda.

"I'm sorry, did you say something about an ex-husband?" Declan asked.

"I did, yes," Mae said. I jumped in.

"He's out of town though. It's kind of a long story, but I know because that's why Wanda had GiGi, her dog, this week. He was out of town visiting his mother. He left a few days ago and isn't set to be home until tomorrow night," I said.

"Okay, thank you. I'll dig into that a little more. If you don't mind waiting here for a few minutes, I'll be right back."

Mae and I both nodded. She pressed her curlers back into my scalp again.

"If it's not Jerry, it's rather convenient that the reigning champion of the Quiche on the Beach Bake Off is murdered only weeks before she's about to clinch her tenth official win, don't you think?" Mae asks.

Mae had a valid point. Maybe Mr. Gordon hated Wanda enough that he didn't want her to be able to revel in the satisfaction of winning the bake off for an entire decade? Or maybe it was possible that someone else had wanted the title bad enough that they'd been willing to kill for it.

CHAPTER FIVE

Ready, Set... Bake Off!

The countdown is on for the annual Quiche on the Beach Bake Off here in Blue Haven. In just three weeks, over a dozen of the area's top contenders will be whisking and baking their way to the prestigious Queen of the Quiche title. Blue Haven will welcome many newcomers for the event who will be ready to give frontrunner Wanda Hemmings a run for her money.

Doris Lions and Patricia Rice are traveling from the mountains of North Carolina to showcase their quiche recipes for the second year in a row, and they're eager to see if they have what it takes to knock Wanda off her throne. Evelyn Hammonds and Dotty Fitzgerald from Bluewater are first-time entries, and let's not forget Suzy Atwater, who has sat comfortably in the runner's-up spot for the last five years. She has a secret ingredient this year that she hopes will help her take home the crown.

If you plan on coming to town for the big event, be sure to make your dinner reservations early and stay tuned right here on Kaffeinated Kitchen: the blog that never disappoints in spilling the latest and greatest culinary secrets from right here in Blue Haven, North Carolina.

Love ya lattes,
Von Reklaw

***

Declan Grant had given me the number of his direct line before he'd let me leave the scene on the morning of Wanda's supposed murder. He'd told me to call if I had any questions or if I thought of anything else that could help with the case. I'd thanked him and a shiver had run through me when my hand had brushed his as I'd pulled the business card from his fingers. Then I'd turned one more time to see Wanda lying on the floor of her cafe before I'd walked out.

Now here I sat, two days later, only a few doors from where it had all happened. Police tape was still stuck like an X over Wanda's front door, but other than that the boardwalk went on as normal. I was sitting under a white umbrella outside Peaches Cafe. I always sat with my back to the wall so that no one would catch a glimpse of what I was writing. The mystery of who Von Reklaw was in this town was what made my blog so intriguing to everyone who lived here. They never knew where Von was or what review s/he'd write up next.

I remembered when my friend Gemma had suggested my pen name. I'd thought she was crazy. Surely someone would be smart enough to figure out that Reklaw was just my real last name spelled backward. But six months in and that mystery was still the talk of the town. I was meticulous when it came to the type of food and restaurant reviews I gave. I made sure that I published most of my visits out of order so that no one could track the posts back to seeing me somewhere the night before. Or, like this one I was currently writing, I showed up to the opening of the new ice cream shop in my short blonde wig with oversized purple sunglasses. Even in a small town where everyone is anyone, gossip still camouflages a woman in a blonde wig. I ordered at the height of a big debate that was going on in the ice cream shop. Suzy Atwater and a few of her crochet group friends were discussing the finale of their favorite book-turned-television-show. Apparently, who ended up with whom was enough to not notice little ole me as I taste-tested a few flavors with a tiny spoon and ordered a double scoop in a waffle cone.

I had just finished my ice cream blog when a few familiar faces sat down around me. I pretended to be busy on my computer while I waited for the one conversation I was sure would break ground shortly. There wasn't a single woman in the crochet club who wouldn't be eager to talk about what had happened to Wanda. They couldn't help it. Town gossip was in their DNA. It took all of seven minutes for the women's conversation to go from how the puff stitch was the perfect scarf stitch to the first Blue Haven murder in, well... *ever*.

"Have you asked her yet?" I heard one woman whisper.

"No, are you crazy?! What if she did do it? I'd be next!" another woman answered. She crossed her legs that were hidden in a pair of purple floral pants and folded her arms over her white, baggy t-shirt.

"Don't you think it's important to know if the head of our crochet group is a murderer?"

I leaned closer to them. My curiosity gave me courage. "Excuse me," I leaned closer to them. "I didn't mean to eavesdrop, but were you talking about the..." I covered the side of my mouth with my hands and finished the sentence, "murder?"

They all gasped. Their hands flew to their chests as if I had just revealed the actual murderer's name.

"Oh dear..." one of them reached over and placed her hand on my shoulder. "You're her! The one who found her. You poor dear."

"Thank you," I said. "It's hard to believe that anyone would want to hurt Wanda." I lied. We all knew the truth, but I wanted more information from them. "Do you think you know who did it?"

I wasn't expecting any of them to be as forward as they were. It must have been the fear I had managed to well up in my eyes combined with the fact that I was the poor dear who'd seen Wanda's body on that tile floor. Once the floodgates opened, they didn't stop.

"Isn't it obvious?" the woman in the floral pants said. "It had to have been Suzy. She was livid when she found out that Wanda had discovered who she was getting her eggs from. Last week Suzy saw her egg farmer outside of Wanda's store. She marched right over there and handed it to them both!"

"And then a week later, boom, she's dead!" I turned to the white-haired lady with thin silver frames covering her eyes as she took over the conversation. "Every week since February when we met to crochet, Suzy would talk about how she was for sure going to win the Quiche on the Beach Bake Off this year with her new eggs."

Wait!" I interrupted. "I thought that Wanda and Farmer Don were in cahoots when it came to eggs?"

"They were," said the white-haired lady, "until a few weeks ago. She got wind that Suzy found a farmer outside of Wilmington with prizewinning eggs."

"Prizewinning?" I asked.

"Seems they've won over the local market up that way. Wanda made a trip up to weasel her way in to start ordering them too. I bet she knew she didn't stand a chance and this was the only way to guarantee her victory."

Suzy Atwater loved being the owner of Peaches Cafe. It had been passed down through two generations and was mostly known for its cakelike waffles, but when it got closer to Quiche on the Beach season Suzy would tease her recipe on the cafe menu. She'd never put the exact one she'd be entering that year on the menu, though; she saved that for the bake off.

First Mae and now the crochet women thought the murder had to do with the upcoming bake off. I had to find out if they were heading in the right direction.

I thanked them all for the information before packing up my stuff and heading off to switch hats from food critic/investigator to dog walker. On the way to my first client of the afternoon, I pulled out my cell phone along with Declan Grant's business card and gave him a call. He'd wanted to hear when I knew something that could help the investigation and boy did I have news for him!

"Special Agent Grant." I paused for a moment to pull myself together when his deep voice answered the phone.

"Agent Grant... I mean Declan, it's Veronica Walker," I said. "I might have some information regarding Wanda's case. Are you up for a little walk around the neighborhood?"

"Well, I did scarf down two vanilla cream donuts for breakfast, so why not?" Declan chuckled.

"Great! Come meet me. I'll text you the address. Give me fifteen minutes," I said.

I didn't give him time to respond. I pulled the phone from my ear and hit the end button as my pace picked up. There's a desolate part of Blue Haven that connects the boardwalk to all the neighborhoods in town. It was the first time since I'd moved to town that I felt somewhat uneasy walking the dirt road by myself. I speed-walked in my strappy tan sandals, and every ten feet or so I'd look back over my shoulder until I came up to the first row of houses on Coastal Court.

A few blocks later I was struggling to catch my breath, and Declan was standing in front of the mailbox of my newest dog walking client. He was dressed less formally today. There was no official detective shirt tucked into his khakis. Instead he had on a cream-colored button-up underneath a burgundy tie. I felt my heart thud against my chest and pretended it was more from the brisk walking than from being able to see Declan's dreamy blue eyes again.

"Good morning Ms. Walker," he said when I was within arm's reach. I shook his hand. He was much taller than I remembered. I had to kink my neck to see his smile.

"Did you find the place okay?" I asked.

"No trouble at all. I'm starting to learn my way around this town."

"Where did you say you were from?" I asked.

I'd known even in a state of shock that Declan was an outsider. He didn't have the can't-miss-it Southern accent that flooded this town. His button-ups and striped ties might be a part of the job, but he was comfortable in them. I could tell that they would be his outfit of choice even off the clock, which was a far cry from the board shorts and swimsuits that made up everyone in Blue Haven's wardrobe.

"I'm originally from Chicago, but I've spent the last ten years in D.C."

"Wow, this must be a culture shock for you," I said.

"It's been an adjustment, but a good one. I needed an escape."

"Were you running from something?" I asked.

Declan's smile faded. His gaze left mine. He looked down at the shiny black toes of his boots before dodging the question.

"Aren't we all?" He winked. "Anyway, to what do I owe the pleasure of your company today?"

"I heard some interesting gossip down at the boardwalk today. I thought it might help with Wanda's case."

Declan followed me down the concrete walkway and up the wooden stairs to the house of Milo Jones. Milo was the town's only lawyer and I had pitched my dog walking services to him on a recent coffee run. He was starting to get busy at the office and he'd agreed that his boxer, Winnie, could use a mid-afternoon walk. I assumed it was the lawyer persona that made Milo one of only two clients I had who locked their doors. I bent down under the potted plant in the far corner of his porch and lifted the clay pot to find the silver key that lay underneath it.

"A group of women who are friends with Suzy Atwater mentioned that she was furious with Wanda. So furious that she actually stormed into Wanda's cafe just last week," I said, turning the key in the lock.

"What was she furious about?" Declan asked.

I pushed open the door and a big, brown, wrinkled forehead came charging at us. Declan and I both bent down and Winnie hopped around in front of us. Her nubby tail wagged as I clipped the metal clasp of the leash onto her purple collar and guided her back out the front door.

"Apparently, Suzy had found a new egg supplier for her cafe. One she thought was for sure going to win her the Quiche on the Beach Bake Off this year. Then last week she saw that same egg supplier dropping off a shipment at Wanda's. The women at the cafe said she was so angry that she ran over and had a spat with both Wanda and the egg farmer."

"That definitely gives her motive."

"I'm having a hard time picturing Suzy doing something so cruel." I paused, thinking back to the day I'd found Wanda. The boardwalk had been quiet. The music from the souvenir shop speakers hadn't been turned on yet. No stores had been open, but when I'd walked into the Savory Egg Cafe to pick up the check, Suzy had already been at her shop. "Suzy had deliveries that morning too. There was not one other person besides the delivery guy anywhere to be found," I said.

"An empty boardwalk gives her opportunity, and a propped-open door certainly gave her the means." Declan said.

He pulled out his notepad and wrote down Suzy's name. I hated the idea of pointing the finger at Suzy. I'd spent many afternoons typing away outside of Peaches Cafe. Suzy would slip me an extra waffle every now and then for my loyalty. It didn't seem possible she'd have it in her to kill someone, and what made it even worse was that I was the one adding her to a suspect list I was happy not to be on.

"I'm going to swing by there later tonight. See if I can get her to crack," Declan said.

"Are you going to go alone?" I asked. I was partly concerned that if Suzy were the killer, she may be determined to keep Declan quiet once she knew he was on to her. The other part of me was quite intrigued with the idea of helping to solve this case. I had a degree in journalism from New York University after all, and my crime blotter job at a dinky NYC paper had made me somewhat qualified to help out. Okay, maybe it didn't, but I was going to tell myself that anyway.

"I can handle it," Declan said.

He seemed unfazed by any possible danger. Even so, I couldn't rightfully let Declan walk into a lion's den alone. Especially since it was my information that was going to put him there. I knew he wouldn't willingly allow me to tag along. That's when I knew I had to come up with my own plan to show up at Peaches Cafe at exactly the right time.

CHAPTER SIX

It was book club night in Blue Haven, which meant that Suzy Atwater would be closing the most popular waffle spot in town at seven sharp to make it on time. Scout and I conveniently went for our after-dinner walk and happened to stroll down the boardwalk a few minutes before seven. Declan was leaning against the wood railing opposite the cafe with his gaze fixed on the beachgoers. Scout and I walked up and I leaned on the railing next to him.

"Fancy seeing you here," I smiled.

"Veronica... what are you—" Scout didn't let him finish. He jumped up and put his front paws on Declan's stomach. I stumbled backward. Scout started barking.

"Scout! No!" I yelled. I yanked his leash to knock him off balance. Once he was back on all fours Declan bent down to his level.

"Hey boy. It's okay," Declan said.

"I am so sorry." I could feel the heat on my cheeks. Chasing after birds were one thing but barking in someone's face was something Scout had never done before.

"Oh, don't worry." Declan patted Scout's head. "He's just protecting you from the big bad stranger."

I laughed. Scout sure knew how to make an impression. His protective demeanor started to subside the more Declan petted him, and soon the barking turned into slobbery kisses. It helped the time go by until the bell on the cafe door rang. We both turned to find Suzy walking out. Her black curls waved in the breeze. She locked the door and tucked the keys into her ankle length green dress. Declan looked over at me.

"You—stay here. I don't want you caught up in this."

I didn't have time to object, but I also wasn't planning on following Declan's direction. I had to know what Suzy had to say. Without being painstakingly obvious, I let Declan walk over to Suzy and while the two of them walked together, Scout and I stayed a few steps behind.

"I appreciate you taking the time to talk to me, Ms. Atwater," Declan said. "I wanted to go over a few things about the day Wanda's body was found. You were here on the boardwalk?"

"Yes. I had a coffee delivery that morning and had to set up the new espresso maker," Suzy said.

"And what time would you say you arrived at the cafe?" Declan asked.

"Some time after seven. Right before the delivery driver arrived," Suzy said.

"Did you happen to notice anything out of the ordinary at that time?"

Suzy took a moment to collect her thoughts, but eventually shook her head and said she'd seen nothing. She usually parked on the opposite side of the boardwalk and wouldn't pass Wanda's shop on the way into work.

"You and Wanda," Declan began, "you argued recently, is that correct?"

"When didn't we?" Suzy confessed. "Look, Mr. Grant, I appreciate your care in this case, but if you think I had anything to do with Wanda's death, you are sadly mistaken."

"Is that right?" I could hear the sarcasm in Declan's voice.

"I'll admit that Wanda and I had our troubles, and I know what the town is saying, but even with our differences I wouldn't kill her over a quiche. I wasn't even sure I should enter the bake off this year. I've been busy working on a new project."

"And what might that be?" Declan asked.

Suzy stopped walking and looked around. When she looked over her shoulder, I slid my sunglasses over my face and spun around. I forgot that I was in the middle of the boardwalk surrounded by tourists. I stopped spinning but my purse didn't and smacked right into the head of a young girl.

"Ow!" she yelled, rubbing the side of her head.

"I'm so sorry," I whispered. "Are you okay?"

She snarled at me and her mother yanked her away with a glare. I apologized again and turned back around to walk with the flow of the crowd. By then, Suzy had made her escape from Declan and he was back to scribbling in his notebook. I walked up to him and peeked over his shoulder. My shadow gave me away.

"I thought I told you to stay put," Declan said.

"I know, I'm sorry. I couldn't help it," I said. "What did you find out?"

"You are a feisty one, aren't you?" Declan asked. I shrugged. I guess I was. "You know I could lose my job for this, but for some strange reason, I trust you."

I felt my cheeks flush at that statement and the way Declan smiled at me. It helped me feel a bit less guilty for knowing he was going against protocol.

"Apparently Suzy is busy working on starting a waffle cart. She said she wasn't even planning on entering the bake off because she has a lot of work to do to get the cart ready by fall."

"Hmmm, that's interesting and contradicts what the crochet group said about the eggs," I said.

"Speaking of eggs—Suzy says that Farmer Don, Wanda's original egg farmer, was quite disgruntled that she switched. She said he too came into the cafe kicking up a storm and even threatened to get even with her."

"Any witnesses?" I asked.

"A whole bunch. It was in the middle of the dinner rush," Declan said.

There was now a second suspect, but Suzy wasn't off the list quite yet. Her story of that day was probable as I remember the delivery truck out by her cafe, but I already knew she was lying about entering the bake off. Von Reklaw had already published the list of entries on Kaffeinated Kitchen and Suzy's name was on it. If she were innocent, why would she lie? I'd have to dig into that later.

"So..." I said. "I guess that means we have a farmer to visit?"

"We?" Declan asked. The two of us were walking in stride.

"What?" I winked. "I have to make a trip to the Farmers Market anyway. Why not stop at Farmer Don's egg stand while I'm at it?"

"Alright, alright," Declan said. "I see you're not going to give up that easily and I'd rather you come with me than do it alone. Meet me there first thing Saturday morning. Until then, no snooping around."

Declan made me shake on it and I figured I'd have to agree to stay on his good side. Not only was he good to look at, but I really did want to figure out if Farmer Don was mad enough at Wanda to want her dead. It made everyone a little uneasy to know that there may be a murderer walking among us.

CHAPTER SEVEN

The Sweetest Shop in Blue Haven is Sweeter Than Ever

If you love cream filling and sprinkles, this is the blog for you! The hardest decision I've ever had to make here in Blue Haven was choosing between the strawberry cheesecake and the chocolate fudge brownie donut from Blue Haven Donuts. Both offer delectable chunks of goodness in each bite and are sure to satisfy even the daintiest of sweet tooths. Thanks to a new special, I no longer have to choose! Two flavors are better than one, and all donut fans will be happy to know that on Fridays at Blue Haven Donuts you can get your second donut half off! This is just another sweet reason to visit our coastal town.

Love ya lattes,
Von Reklaw

***

It was the day before I was to meet Declan at the Farmers Market and I had no dogs to walk, but I did have two very important tasks to check off my list. The sun was hiding behind the clouds and it was the perfect day to photograph what I needed for my blog. I had to be careful of being recognized, so I had to put on my Von Reklaw outfit. I tucked my hair under a short blonde wig and slid oversized sunglasses over my eyes to make sure everything still looked good. Scout snarled the entire way down the stairs wondering who this stranger was in his house. I calmed him down with a treat and pulled the wig off my head before heading out the door. I'd do a quick change in the private showers near the beach where I'd been successful at not being noticed a few times before.

My phone rang on the way to the boardwalk. It was my father. I had purposely been ignoring both his and my mother's phone calls since Wanda's murder. I wasn't ready to tell them about it because I knew they'd be worried. My dad would probably be on the next flight down. I took a deep breath and tried to act calm.

"Hi, Daddy," I said.

"Oh thank goodness, you're alive! Your mother and I were getting nervous," he said. "What have you been up to?"

My voice cracked as I tried to laugh off his comment. *Don't worry, Dad, it's not me that's dead. Though I did recently discover a body and now I'm a witness to a murder investigation.* That conversation went well in my head.

"I've been... busy." Those were the words that came out instead. "My dog walking business is growing. I also redecorated the sunroom and finished painting the office. I'll have to send pictures soon."

"That's exciting news. Your grandmother would be so proud. How's the writing going?"

My dad had always been my biggest fan. He was more into risk-taking than my mother was. When my grandmother had left me her farmhouse, my mother hadn't been too keen on me leaving my stable, paying job to move to North Carolina. She'd asked what I would do and I'd told her that I would figure it out when I got here. The first subscriber to my blog had been my dad and he'd been reading every post since. He had been careful not to comment so no one in this town would know who was behind it. My grandmother had been a big name in Blue Haven and residents would have recognized his last name immediately.

"The writing is coming along. I'm on my way to do a little now. How'd you like my last post? I know you love those cream-filled donuts."

"Oh Von, I loved it! I can't wait until your mom and I come down in a couple of months. The donut shop will be my first stop."

My dad has been calling me Von since before I could walk. Veronica wasn't the easiest name for a child to pronounce, so my dad had tried to make it easier with a nickname. It had stuck for the last three decades of my life. When I'd created my blog alias and told him the name I was going to use, he'd been ecstatic. I think he'd liked that he'd had a hand in my fresh start.

"I can't wait to see you!"

I was secretly hoping this whole murder investigation would be cleared up by then. That way when he did find out, I could let him know that everything was fine. I decided to hold off on telling my Dad about Wanda until our next conversation. He was so excited about how good things were going that I didn't want to throw a wrench in it.

"I have to go, Dad. Got to get to work. I love you."

"I love you too, Von." My dad hung up first and I silenced my phone before slipping it back into my purse and ducking into the shower before heading to my next assignment.

My stomach was growling as I pulled the door open at Blue Haven Donuts. I'd stopped here many times before as my actual self. Their pumpkin cream-filled donuts were my favorite, but today I was here for the newest addition to their menu—the cherry cream cheese-filled donut with an almond glaze.

I'd timed my arrival perfectly. The morning crowd had cleared, but the afternoon rush was yet to come, which meant there were plenty of donuts left for me. I always had to order more than what I was reviewing so as not to make it obvious, and my ordering tactic was perfection by now.

"Good morning, how can I help you today?" Jared, the young man behind the counter, was home from his first year of college. He had been working at Blue Haven Donuts since before he could drive. I'd met him when he'd come home for spring break. He was quite the chatterbox. I almost asked how his first year of college had gone but caught myself before I could reveal my true identity. I pulled a blank piece of paper from my pocket and pretended to read from it.

"I need a dozen donut holes, any assortment, an apple fritter, a chocolate creme, and two of your new cherry cream cheese donuts. If you don't mind, could you put the cherry donuts in a separate bag? The boss hates when his donuts touch other flavors," I winked.

"You got it," Jared said. He rang up my order and started piling it into separate bags.

I slipped him some cash, let him keep the change, and headed back to the private shower areas at the beach for another quick change. I hid Von and the donuts in my oversized bag and snuck out as good old Veronica before anyone noticed. It was time for the next task on my to-do list.

I went back to the donut shop line again and ordered a few more donut holes so I didn't look funny sitting outside on the patio. I found an empty table closest to the boardwalk and sat alone until I heard a familiar bark. I looked up to see GiGi down at my feet. I followed her leash to the manly hands that were holding it and stood up to introduce myself.

"You must be Jerry," I said. "I'm Veronica. It's a pleasure to meet you."

"Likewise," Jerry said.

His grip was firm. What was left of his salt and pepper hair caught the morning breeze. He slid the chair out from the other side of the table, and when he sat down GiGi hopped up into his lap. I was happy to see she was adjusting well.

"My condolences again about Wanda," I said.

Jerry was the last person I'd expected a call from when the unknown number had come up on my phone the other day. He had objected to the idea of a dog walker when Wanda had first hired me, but now that she was gone, he was open to discussions. Those had been his exact words.

"Thank you," Jerry said. "Wanda always spoke very highly of you. She said you took good care of GiGi. Now that she's gone, I think I may need a little help on my long days at the office."

I nodded. It was shocking to hear that Wanda had spoken highly of me. Especially after she'd threatened to take her business elsewhere because of Scout's antics.

"I am happy to help in any way I can." I pulled out my planner and flipped it open to the month overview page. "What days are you looking for?"

"Monday and Thursday afternoons through the rest of the month would be best for right now. The other days, my... assistant will be helping."

I jotted Gigi's name down in the open spots and tried not to show my curiosity about the way he'd fidgeted when mentioning his assistant. I wondered if that was the way he referred to his old mistress/new girlfriend.

"Wonderful. I've got GiGi down. I usually give a two-hour window. I will be there anytime between noon and two o'clock in the afternoon. You would qualify for the multi-day discount I offer. I accept cash and check right now, with payment due on the first day of service for the week," I said.

"Yes, I'm aware. It'll be on the counter when you come in. Here's the address." Jerry slid a piece of paper over to me. "I hate to chat and run, but I am being beckoned to the police station."

"The police station?" I asked.

"It's a waste of time, if you ask me. They already dragged me down there earlier this week. My mother has fallen ill and I went to Atlanta to visit her. The facility has already confirmed my attendance," he scoffed. "If you ask me, this is an open and shut case. Suzy Atwater has always had it in for Wanda. Not sure what else they need from me."

"Well, good luck. Hopefully they don't keep you too long. It's a beautiful day," I said.

I pulled out my laptop and sat out on the patio of the donut shop for a little while after Jerry left. I was confident Jerry wouldn't be at the station long. A lot of fingers seemed to be pointing to Suzy Atwater. Her conversation with Declan hadn't exactly cleared her name, and like Mae had said, with Wanda out of the way this was Suzy's chance to win the crown she'd always wanted. Farmer Don may be inching closer on the list, but Suzy was still the top suspect.

I took a break from typing and looked up right as Dotty Fitzgerald was walking by Blue Haven Donuts. A large straw hat and dark glasses made it hard to recognize her, but I'd been over to her bakery in Bluewater enough times to recognize the fiery red strands that fell to her shoulders and the lipstick that matched. Dotty had moved down to Bluewater from New Hampshire about ten years ago. She'd had enough of the frigid winters. When her husband passed away she'd decided there was no more time to waste and had fulfilled her dream of opening a bakery. We had spent many of my visits chatting about the Northeast.

"Hi Dotty!" I waved. Dotty jumped at the sound of her name and looked in my direction. She slid her glasses down until her green eyes were staring straight at me.

"Veronica? Is that you?" Dotty whispered. I nodded. She crept her high heels closer to me. "I didn't recognize you without that four-legged friend of yours."

I laughed. Dotty had only seen me once with Scout, but he'd left a lasting impression by lifting his leg on the wheel of her two-door coupe. Most people recognize Scout before me when we're out and about.

"What brings you over to Blue Haven?" I asked.

Dotty swallowed hard and I watched as the redness grew in her cheeks. The silence cut between us harder than the wind blowing off the ocean. Dotty was never at a loss for words. I wondered if it had to do with the Quiche on the Beach Bake Off. Was she also about to steal Suzy's new egg farmer?

"I'm just—err—running some errands," she stuttered.

It was hard to believe that, the way her fingers were twitching at her hips. I didn't push. Dotty's daily activities were none of my business. Unless... no way—my mind started to scream. Was Dotty coming back to cover her tracks? Could she have killed Wanda?

CHAPTER EIGHT

The Greenmarket near Lincoln Center had been one of my favorite escapes while living in New York City. I'd sneak out from the newspaper on a Thursday afternoon with Gemma in tow. We'd stock up on fresh vegetables and baked goods. I'd stuff my face with a croissant while walking through Central Park.

I missed days like that on occasion here in Blue Haven. Mostly, I missed Gemma. She had always known what to do or say when I needed advice, and with everything going on here with Wanda's death, I could have used her. Today I was going to have to settle for a new Farmers Market partner. One who was tall and handsome and maybe made my heart flutter when he leaned in a little too close.

Declan was waiting at the black iron gate by the entrance to the market when I walked up with Scout in hand. *Turn on your detective face*, I whispered to myself, trying to hide the flushed cheeks I knew were forming.

"Good morning, Ms. Walker," Declan said.

"Good morning to you," I managed to say back in a very professional tone. In Declan's hand he held two green fabric bags. He tucked them under his arm as he bent down to scratch Scout's ears. There was no barking today. Declan was very good at winning people—or I guess I should say pets—over.

"I see you're ready to do some shopping," I said, pointing to the bags under his arm.

"I sure am." Declan waved his hand in front of him. "Shall we?"

I nodded.

Farmer Don's egg stand was at the opposite end of the market from the entrance, so we decided to do our shopping first, and interrogate him later. In true Veronica-from-New-York fashion, I stopped first at the local bakery table and stocked up on croissants. With lots of early morning dog walking this week, it would be the perfect breakfast on the go. I of course grabbed an extra one for the appetite I was working up after strolling through the market. Even a handsome detective wasn't going to keep me from each rich, buttery bite.

"That looks delicious," Declan said. I handed my credit card to the girl behind the register.

"Oh, you have no idea. Ms. Allie makes some of the best in town."

"Alright, that's it. You've convinced me."

Declan grabbed a few croissants of his own and then we headed down the aisle again to see what else we could find. The next stop happened to be much more than both of us had expected. As we strolled past the crates of tomatoes stacked up on a long table, Mae from the candle shop was deep in conversation with Betty Jean. Betty Jean had probably been the only person in this town who would have considered Wanda Hemmings a friend. Being that they'd been neighbors for more than thirty years, some nights when I'd walked Scout after dinner I'd seen them sitting out on Betty Jean's porch sipping their glasses of sweet tea.

Declan and I looked at each other and both of our eyes shot open wide. We slowed our pace and took a sudden interest in cherry tomatoes. Declan picked through each basket pretending to examine them while I stepped closer to Betty Jean.

"I wouldn't be surprised if Linda were behind it." Betty Jean never had understood the idea of whispering. Everyone within ten feet could hear every word.

"Linda? Why do you say that?" Mae asked.

"Oh please, it's no secret why Wanda and Jerry's marriage fell apart. Wanda told me that she went to bring him dinner one late night at the office and she walked in on Jerry. He was in the middle of enjoying something, or should I say, *someone* else."

"No!" Mae threw her hand over her mouth.

"Poor Wanda," Betty Jean said. "I'd always wondered how someone as charismatic as Jerry could be married to someone like Wanda. Any time I saw the two of them together they both looked miserable, but she certainly didn't deserve to walk in on her husband and his dental hygienist. What a shame!"

I stayed as close to Betty Jean as I could. I wanted to soak in every part of their conversation. Linda and I hadn't had any run-ins since I'd moved to town so I knew very little about her other than that she worked for Jerry.

"But why would Linda want to kill Wanda if she won Jerry in the end?" Mae asked.

"Well, I happen to know that even though Jerry and Wanda's divorce was finalized over two months ago, Jerry still stopped by now and then for a little midnight rendezvous. The last time was only two days before Wanda died."

"Wait a minute. You're telling me that Wanda and Jerry were still sleeping together? I thought they hated each other." Mae scratched the top of her head.

"That's what she wanted everyone to think. A woman like Wanda couldn't let the town know any of her weaknesses. Wanda and Jerry didn't agree on much, but when it came to what they did in the bedroom, that was one of the things they both could agree on."

"So, if Linda found out Jerry was still sleeping with Wanda..." Mae said.

"She would definitely want to take a whack at her," Betty Jean said.

My hand was frozen around a ripe tomato as Betty Jean and Mae finished their conversation. I turned to Declan who was subtly waving me away from them. I loosened my grip and moved slowly out into the aisle where Declan was standing.

"Did you hear that?" Declan asked.

"I sure did," I said. "I never would've thought Wanda would be someone to lose her life by the hands of a jilted lover."

"I guess we have another suspect to add to our list."

"I guess we do," I said.

The chiming of my phone interrupted our conversation. I reached down into my purse and my hand tried to find my phone amid house keys, lip gloss, a tissue pack, and dozens of irrelevant receipts. When I finally felt it, I pulled it out to see Gemma's name flash across the screen. I hadn't spoken to her since before I'd found Wanda's body, and I knew once I told her about it that this conversation would be much longer than any I could have while browsing the Farmers Market. I hit the silence button even though I knew I'd get an earful for it later.

Declan and I stopped at a couple of fruit stands where I grabbed a few baskets of blueberries and strawberries, and then we made our way to Farmer Don's egg stand. We waited a few minutes until the line cleared and each of us picked up a carton of eggs. I wasn't sure how Declan planned on bringing up the subject of Wanda, but I let him take the lead when we got to the register.

"I hear these fine eggs make an award-winning quiche," Declan said. He placed his carton on the table and fiddled in his pocket to find his wallet.

"They sure used to," Farmer Don huffed.

"I bet it made you pretty angry when good ole Wanda switched suppliers, huh?" I jumped in.

"Wouldn't you be angry? For almost ten years that woman has been basking in victory thanks to *my* eggs. Then suddenly, she thinks she can do better? Hah! I was counting down the days until the bake off just so I could watch her crumble."

Declan and I looked at each other. Wanda losing the bake off would be a great victory for Farmer Don. Killing her before the big event didn't seem like the smartest idea, but maybe he'd been so angry he hadn't cared. Farmer Don had also run the risk of Wanda winning the bake off, and that would've been death to his egg business. He could've returned to her cafe to try and convince her to switch back to him and things might have gotten out of hand.

"Unfortunately, that's impossible now," Declan said. He handed over his credit card. "She's dead."

"Yes, I heard," Farmer Don said. He started typing into his register. "That woman had it coming to her. She burned so many bridges that eventually she was going to feel the flames."

"I don't suppose it was your bridge?" Declan asked.

"Oh, you'd like that, wouldn't you?" Farmer Don's voice grew terse. "The big bad detective who solves the first ever murder here in Blue Haven. Too bad that while Wanda was lying on the cold floor of her cafe, I was twenty miles outside town feeding my chickens."

His brows furrowed and his fingers began to pound at the keys. That's when I noticed a few scratches on the top of his right hand. They looked like they were in the middle of the healing process, but fresh enough that they could be from Wanda. Maybe she clawed him in the middle of their scuffle.

"Do you have anyone who can corroborate your story?" Declan asked.

"Yeah, three dozen of my white feathered friends. I think you two have wasted enough of my time for today."

Farmer Don slid Declan's eggs into his bag and threw his credit card back across the table. I decided I didn't need a dozen eggs anymore and left mine where I'd found them. Declan thanked Farmer Don for his time, but there was no response. Scout was getting antsy by then anyway and was beginning to pull me toward the exit. When we were no longer in earshot of the large market crowd, I put my detective hat back on.

"Did you see the scratches on his hand?" I asked.

"I did. We know there was some kind of altercation by the rips on Wanda's shirt, but there was no DNA found under her fingernails," Declan said.

"So, what do you think?" I asked.

"I definitely can't rule him off the suspect list yet. He had motive, means, opportunity, and no real alibi. I mean any farmer can say they were feeding their chickens, but no chicken is going to help back that up."

I laughed at the thought of a clucking chicken trying to Morse code an alibi. It certainly would help Farmer Don, but Declan was right. Farmer Don had to stay on the suspect list, which thanks to Betty Jean now had another name on it. This case was becoming more interesting by the minute. With the evidence stacking up, it was getting clear that Special Agent Parks was on to something. Wanda's death had been no accident.

"What do you say we put the detective work away for a bit and enjoy one of these?" Declan reached down into his paper bag and pulled out one of his croissants. My stomach was instantly reminded that I hadn't eaten anything since I'd woken up.

"I say let's do it!"

The two of us, with Scout in tow, found and sat down at an empty picnic table. Scout lay down underneath the bench I was sitting on. I yanked my croissant out of the bag and took a bite.

"Mmm, I forgot how good these were," I said in between bites.

"This reminds me of a patisserie I frequented in Virginia," Declan said.

"I thought you said you came from D.C.?" I asked.

"I did. I lived in Virginia. I took the metro daily into D.C. for work."

I'd forgotten how D.C. related to New York City. My parents had commuted from Westchester County for most of my childhood. The city was work for them and vacation for me. I think that's why I'd found it so fascinating. I'd gotten to take the train in for Christmas festivities and Broadway shows. The allure of the tall buildings had me hooked. I'd counted down the days until I graduated for me to be able to call it home.

"Did you like it? Working in D.C.? I asked.

"Yeah, for a while. The commute kind of got old. The on-call rarely ended. It made it hard for the things I wanted most. When this spot opened, my team thought I was crazy. I didn't expect a murder the first week on the job, but I have to get paid for something."

"What kind of things did you want?" I asked.

"Oh, you know: wife, family, a house with a yard."

I smiled. Declan shoved the last piece of his croissant into his mouth. I was kind of surprised by his response. For some reason I didn't picture him as a family man. Maybe it was all those TV shows where the crime scene detective is always on an airplane leaving their significant other behind and eventually it all ends in divorce. I could see why Declan chose Blue Haven now. Wanda's murder was one in a million; it'd probably be another hundred years before there was another case like this here.

I bent down to pull my water bottle from my purse. My fingers wrapped around the metal top and I grimaced as I twisted the tightly wound cap off and drank down a cold sip of water. Betty Jean and Mae were walking in my direction and for some reason my first instinct was to hide. I turned my head and slid my hand over the side of my face. Declan's eyes squinted at my motion. I could tell by the way his shoulders stiffened that I had made him uncomfortable. I wasn't embarrassed to be seen with Declan. He was closer to my age than anyone else in this town. Sitting with him would probably seem normal, but for some reason I felt as if I would be judged. It wouldn't be long until I found out.

"Veronica, it's nice to see you again dear." Betty Jean's high-pitched voice yelled out. "How lovely to see you, too, Mr. Grant."

"Please, call me Declan. It's a pleasure to see you, too, Betty Jean. It looks like you had a successful day at the market." He pointed at the multiple bags of vegetables she was holding in her hand.

"I look forward to Saturday mornings at the market every week," she said. "I didn't realize you two knew each other."

Declan looked over at me and I could tell by his straight lipped smile that he wanted me to take over the conversation. Another long sip of water gave me enough time to think. I'm sure Betty Jean knew by now that I was the one who'd found Wanda.

"We don't, really," I said. "Declan is the lead detective on Wanda's case and he had a few additional questions since I... well..."

"Found her body." Betty Jean finished the sentence for me. I nodded. "You poor dear."

"Any suspects yet?" Mae chimed in. "It's unnerving going to bed at night knowing there's a murderer in this town. I sleep alone, you know." Mae winked in Declan's direction.

Declan rubbed his hand over his mouth to hide his amusement. I could tell he found the humor in Mae's intrigue with his detective work. In a town like Blue Haven everyone wanted to know everything, all the time. Crap! I was turning into one of those small towners. Look at me, piggy backing on Declan's detective work. At least I had a leg up on Mae. I was a journalist. Okay, I was a food blogger, but since Wanda's death could have a serious impact on the Quiche on the Beach Bake Off, one of the biggest reasons people read my blog, I had the right to stick my nose in this. That's what I was going to tell myself anyway as I listened to Declan's response.

"It's an active investigation," Declan said. "We have some leads and hope to close the book on this case soon."

"I sure hope so," Mae said. "We have the utmost faith in you, Mr. Grant. I should be going. It's almost time to open up the store."

"I should be going too," Betty Jean said. "I'll walk out with you, Mae. You two enjoy your date."

Betty Jean winked. My jaw dropped open, but she spun around before I had time to spit out an objection. I stared at her and Mae as they walked towards the iron gates that led to the parking lot. By that time Scout was starting to get restless. He had wrapped his leash around my ankles. When I finally untangled him he put his paws on the bench and snatched the rest of the croissant from my hands.

"Scout," I yelled. I could hear Declan laughing as he watched from the other side of the table. "What a waste of a good croissant."

"It wasn't a waste," Declan chimed in. "You know he savored every bit of that."

"I guess." I tapped Scout on the nose with my finger, but it didn't faze him. "I should get going. He's getting antsy and I have to get to work," I said.

"Oh yeah, of course." Declan stood from the table and shoved his hands into his pocket. "I—um—I had fun with you. It's not often I'm in such good company while on assignment," he said.

"Same," I said. "I mean, I'm usually in good company, but it's nice to be around someone who walks on two legs and can talk back with actual words."

The two of us laughed. We hung around the parking lot for a couple more minutes before Scout had had enough. He started whining and I took that as a cue to stop acting like a teenager standing in front of her first crush. I said goodbye and walked the whole way home wearing the smile Declan had given me.

CHAPTER NINE

Join the Coolest Kids in Blue Haven at This Popular Saturday Hangout

For those of you renting beach houses on your visit to Blue Haven, I have the perfect place to go to stock your fridge! The Blue Haven Farmers Market has over two dozen of the area's best local goods. You will find anything from local honey and homemade almond milk to the best grass-fed beef and farm fresh eggs this side of North Carolina! You'll find every color of the rainbow at the market when it comes to fruits and vegetables.

The Blue Haven Farmers Market is open from Thursday through Sunday during peak season. If you're coming on a Saturday, be sure to set your alarm clocks early, though, because most vendors sell out within the first couple of hours.

I'll be sharing some amazing recipes from my Farmers Market shopping list in future blog posts so don't forget to subscribe, and thanks for shopping local!

Love ya lattes,
Von Reklaw

***

I was semi-distracted when I arrived home from the Farmers Market, by Betty Jean's assumption that Declan and I had been on a date. Especially after my convincing story about him questioning me about Wanda's death. I indulged in another croissant to calm my nerves before I sat down to write another blog. This time I had to write about what everyone was thinking. Was the Quiche on the Beach Bake Off still going to happen? It was a question I had sent from my Von Reklaw email to the town's event committee the day after Wanda's murder. They had finally responded.

Dear Ms. Reklaw,

We are delighted that you are looking forward to covering the Quiche on the Beach event this year! We have spoken with the Blue Haven Police Department and the contestants of the bake off. As of right now, there doesn't seem to be any reason not to go forward as we believe that this event is the bright light this town needs right now. We will be working very closely with the town and will make a final decision as the event draws near.

Sincerely,

Adam Jones
Event Director

I fell back into my chair with a smile. Adam Jones was right: Blue Haven needed this. The businesses relied on the influx of tourists. This was also the big ten-year celebration and as sad as it was to think about it, there was also a little intrigue in knowing that there was going to be a new winner. I closed out of Adam Jones's email and pulled up my blog page to start typing.

Blue Haven can rest easy tonight. The Quiche on the Beach Bake Off is set to go on as planned—for the time being. That means that all of your tastebuds can continue to count down in hopes that they will get to indulge in the magnificent recipes of eight of the area's finest chefs.

If the bake off does go forward, this year will be different—without a doubt. I have to wonder if Wanda would have wanted us all to enjoy the bake off as she did. Wanda Hemmings loved the Quiche on the Beach event. As she was the reigning champion, it's easy to see why. But this year I'd like to send a reminder: when you're plunging your fork into your fluffy slice of quiche, remember what this event brings to the town you all love. This masterful recipe that Blue Haven has become so famous for is about more than a trophy. It's about the laughter, the community, and everyone coming together.

With that being said, get your forks ready! I hope to see you very soon.

Love ya lattes,
Von Reklaw

I was dragging photos into my blog layout when my phone rang. I looked over to see Gemma's name again. If I sent her to voicemail twice in one day, I'd never live it down. The blog was going to have to take a backseat.

"Hey, Gemma!" I said.

"Veronica Walker, where have you been?"

"I know, I know! You are not going to believe what's going on down here," I said.

I pushed the keyboard to the side of my desk and propped my feet up. Gemma loved all things true crime. We used to watch marathons of those types of shows in our little top floor apartment. She'd even started a podcast about unsolved crimes that had taken place in the New York area. I had to be careful about what I told Gemma, but maybe her sleuthing skills could help.

"I'm in the middle of solving a murder," I said.

"A *what?*"

"Well, at least the police think it's a murder. I'm pretty sure they're not wrong. I walked into a cafe the other day to pick up my dog walking paycheck and found a dead body on the floor."

"*Seriously?* That's terrifying," Gemma said. "What was it like? Seeing a dead body?"

"Honestly, I was so petrified that I can't even remember. I saw the body and then I screamed. I don't remember much else other than being questioned by police once they arrived."

"Questioned?" Gemma asked. "Like, you're a suspect?"

Thankfully, my time as a suspect had been miniscule. One I never want to experience again. With the suspect list growing by the day, I had all but been forgotten. Unless Declan was keeping me close to see if I made any wrong moves. Wow. That was the first time I'd ever thought about my time with Declan in that way. Could he be keeping tabs on me? Playing along with my search of the suspect to see if I slipped up? I sure hope not.

"I wouldn't call myself a suspect," I said. "At least, I don't think so. Anyway, it's pretty much the talk of the town these days and somehow I've inserted myself in the investigation."

"I'm so jealous! You're down there solving a crime and I'm up here reporting on the latest rat-infested restaurant closures." Gemma let out a sigh so loud I had to pull the phone from my ear.

"Sounds like you need a vacation. I have plenty of empty bedrooms in Nana's farmhouse."

Before I'd even finished my sentence Gemma was on the computer looking for the next flight out of JFK. It's funny how Gemma had spent the last six months trying to convince me to move back to New York City and now she couldn't wait to get out. Let alone being willing to come to the small town of Blue Haven.

"There's a nonstop leaving tomorrow morning. I could be there by eleven. Does that work for you?" Gemma asked.

"Oh wow, you weren't kidding," I said. I flipped through the pages of my planner. "Eleven it is. I'll be there to pick you up."

"Awesome! I'm going to get packing then. See you in the morning!"

A click followed. Gemma coming to Blue Haven was the last thing I'd expected, but as it would turn out, Gemma's arrival was going to be helpful when it came to crossing names off the suspect list.

CHAPTER TEN

Scout sure was happy when we ran into Mr. Gordon on our way to get morning coffee. His fluffy tail wagged with each step we took, and he couldn't stop himself from galloping along as close to Mr. Gordon as he could get. Scout had always been fond of him. The day I'd arrived to unpack the minimal things I'd taken with me from New York City, Scout had somehow escaped the yard and run right onto Mr. Gordon's porch. After a frantic few minutes of calling his name, I'd heard a raspy voice yell from outside the picket fence. I'd looked over to find Mr. Gordon pointing to Scout. He was lying paws up, next to a rocking chair, basking in the morning sun. They must've bonded that day.

"So, I heard you've been hanging out a lot with that handsome detective," Mr. Gordon said. "That's what the ladies at water aerobics are calling him."

I looked over at him wide eyed. My cheeks were already warm from the sun, but suddenly they felt like I was standing near a fire.

"I don't think I'd call it *hanging out*. We've bumped into each other a few times. I tried to drill him for info on the investigation into Wanda's death."

"Does he have anything so far? That woman had a lot of enemies. I can't imagine it'd be easy," he said.

"He wouldn't budge. His lips are sealed," I lied.

I didn't want to let on that I knew anything. Declan was pushing the envelope enough letting me tag along—or I guess I should say, not arresting me for sticking my nose a little further into his business than I should.

"Have you heard about Linda Travis?" Mr. Gordon asked. He was too eager to wait for an answer. "She's apparently the mistress that broke up Jerry and Wanda's marriage. Betty Jean saw Jerry's car pulling down Wanda's street pretty late a couple nights before she was murdered. She said they still had midnight rendezvous. Perhaps Linda found out."

"That's definitely a possibility," I said. "I'm sure Special Agent Grant will check that out."

"You have beautiful eyes." The comment came out of nowhere. Mr. Gordon's stare hung to mine. "My wife had emerald eyes like yours. She and your grandmother were two peas in a pod."

"I remember," I said.

I've always regretted not visiting my grandmother as much when I was older. I was pinching pennies in New York City and too proud to ask to borrow money for a plane ticket. Work had also kept me busy; even though it had been mundane, it at least had paid my bills. Even with a busy schedule, there never was a Thursday that went by that I hadn't called her. She would catch me up on the stories of her week, and Mr. Gordon's wife, Rose, had somehow always found her way into them.

Rose and my grandmother had never missed Monday night bingo at the town hall. They'd baked sugar cookies for every holiday and my grandmother would tell me how Mr. Gordon would get yelled at for sneaking one or two when they weren't looking.

Rose had passed away a few years before my grandmother. I could hear the loneliness in my grandmother's voice after she was gone. Even with her weekly visits to check on Mr. Gordon and carrying on bingo traditions, it hadn't been the same. I like to think the two of them are somewhere now, serving up sugar cookies and staring at their bingo boards waiting for the next combination to be called out.

"You remind me of her sometimes," Mr. Gordon said. "She loved mysteries. If Rose were still here, she'd be standing next to you right now trying to figure out the next clue. She'd be determined to solve this case. I bet you'll do it before the police."

"Haha, I don't know about that," I said.

"I do. You're a smart cookie."

I let out another chuckle and watched Mr. Gordon slide his glasses back over the top of his nose. We were finally at the boardwalk. Lattes All Day had a line outside their window, but lucky for me I'd put in my order this time before I left the house.

"Well, this is me," I pointed.

"I suppose it is. You have a wonderful day, Veronica."

I watched as Mr. Gordon bent down in slow motion to meet Scout. He patted the top of Scout's head and didn't flinch when Scout shook himself and smacked his ears against Mr. Gordon's chest. He grabbed the railing beside him to stand back up, tipped his hat and began to walk to the other end of the boardwalk.

"You enjoy those pancakes!" I yelled, before squeezing past the line to the to-go order window.

I grabbed my coffee and laid down some cash for my tab. There was enough time to get Scout back home, hop in the car and get to the airport to pick up my long-lost friend—and not to my surprise, the soon-to-be newest sleuth in Blue Haven.

***

Ten minutes after the time Gemma's flight was supposed to land she was wheeling her suitcase through the double doors from the airport baggage claim. My name pierced my ears as it rolled off her tongue and I waved frantically as her heels trotted on the pavement and her auburn hair waved in the wind.

"I am so happy to see you!" Gemma squealed when she was close enough to throw her arms around me. "I cannot wait for you to show me the new world you live in and tell me all about this—" she covered the side of her lips with her palm and whispered, "—murder investigation."

"It's been an interesting couple weeks," I said. "I'm so glad you're here."

I grabbed the handle to the car's backseat and pulled the door open for Gemma to place her luggage. I was shocked at the fact that she'd managed to fit everything into one suitcase. Gemma's purse alone was usually stuffed to the brim with her daily necessities.

I walked back around to the driver's side. Gemma slid into the passenger seat and pulled her iridescent framed sunglasses over her face. She pulled the visor down and spread a neutral color across her lips. My seatbelt was barely fastened before she started digging.

"Okay, tell me everything," she said.

"Where do I even start?" I said. I turned over my shoulder and waited for the traffic to pass before I pulled out of the pick-up lane to the road that would lead us back to Blue Haven. "I walked in on a dead body. The suspect list is growing, but there's still not enough evidence to lock someone away."

"I can imagine the police in this town are freaking out. I mean, when was the last time there was a murder here?" Gemma asked.

"Never," I said. "There are crime scene investigators in this town, though. I had no idea, but I've been working closely with one named Declan Grant. Working might be a bit exaggerated, but he's tolerating my eagerness."

"Oh—is he cute?" Gemma snapped her eyes in my direction.

I didn't answer right away. I mean, of course I thought Declan was good looking, but I knew if I admitted that, Gemma would be the first to play matchmaker. She'd always been like that. It was how I'd met Jonathan, my loser ex-boyfriend. We'd gone to the off-Broadway show he'd been starring in and, after drooling over him for the entire two-hour show, Gemma had been determined to introduce us. When she had, there'd been an instant connection. Unfortunately, Jonathan hadn't told me that he'd already had a connection with his co-star and he'd been seeing us both at the same time.

That heartbreak had come right before losing my Nana and I couldn't help but think that this was her way of pointing me toward my next chapter in life where I'd just so happened to meet Declan Grant.

"I mean, he's not really my type." That was only a partial lie. I didn't know him enough to know if he was my type, but so far he was leaning in that direction.

"Bummer! Okay, let's go through the suspects," Gemma insisted.

"There is Suzy Atwater. She's another cafe owner and she's been runner-up to Wanda at the Quiche on the Beach Bake Off for the last five years. She's working on opening a new business, so she said she's been super busy, but I'm pretty sure she lied about being too busy to enter this year's contest because her name is on the competitor list that I, or should I say, Von Reklaw, received from the town event committee."

"Von Reklaw, I love it! I'm so glad your food critic blog has become such a success."

"Me too," I said.

"Okay, so who's next?" Gemma asked.

"Farmer Don was not happy with Wanda. She'd been using his eggs for her quiches for over a decade. Recently, she switched to a new egg farmer. He has no real alibi for the day Wanda's body was found. And then there's Linda Travis, Wanda's ex-husband's mistress. It seems that Wanda and her ex were still getting busy under the sheets even though he's supposed to be with Linda now."

"Ohhh yes, a crime of passion." Gemma pulled out her phone. "What does Linda Travis have to say?"

"I don't know yet." I tapped the handle to turn on the blinker for the Blue Haven exit. "I haven't had a chance to eavesdrop. To be honest, I've never even met Linda, which is surprising since it takes all of a day to meet everyone who lives in this town."

Leave it up to Gemma to devise a full-blown plan of attack before we'd even crossed the town line. We were stopped at the red light off the exit when she turned her phone to me. Linda Travis's social media profile was staring back at me. Her blonde curly hair and hazel eyes were front and center.

"Looks like Linda loves her some yoga at Mindful Heart Yoga. Do you know where that is?"

"Oh, yes, I do! It's in the town next to us, over in Bluewater."

Gemma looked at me. "Really? What's the next town after that? Bluebird?" We both laughed.

"Oh look! She's checked in the last four Monday's in a row for their 7 am class. What do you say?"

The fact that we were already pulling up to the farmhouse shows how small a town Blue Haven was. I put the car in park and looked curiously at Gemma. She couldn't possibly have suggested the two of us sign up for yoga with Linda Travis. I haven't taken a single yoga class in my life. She was crazy.

"Yoga? I'll be the next in this town to drop dead if you sign me up for that."

"Oh, come on, Veronica! It'll be fun. Besides, I can't let you have all the fun playing detective, and what better place for women to catch up on gossip than their yoga class? Please?"

Gemma squeezed her phone in between her palms and raised them to her chest. She jutted out her bottom lip and blinked her exhaustingly long eyelashes in my direction. I gave in.

"Fine," I said. "Sign us up."

I could hear Declan's voice in the back of my mind as I agreed to Gemma's crazy scheme. "I don't want you to get caught up in this." Boy, was he going to give me an earful when he found out.

CHAPTER ELEVEN

These Are the Best Places to Grab a Coffee in Blue Haven!

Did you know you could spend an entire week in Blue Haven and not sip the same coffee twice? The Blue Haven boardwalk is blessed to have so many amazing coffee choices. Here are my recommendations for how to go about having the best coffee adventure.

On Sundays you get a free coffee with every donut purchased at Blue Haven Donuts. That's a no-brainer. Kick your Monday off at Lattes All Day, because that's the day you can get a free refill after 4 pm. Bring your appetite on a Tuesday to Peaches Cafe. They offer twofers on their coffee so be sure to bring a friend. On Wednesday be sure to stop at Benny's Pancake House because, well, you can't leave Blue Haven without saying you went to Benny's. Thursdays are definitely meant for Sid's Soda Shop, where you can try the town's famous vanilla coffee float. On Friday you don't even have to leave your beach towel, because the coffee wagon will come to you, and of course on Saturday you'll find The Ground Coffee Truck while you shop the market.

Seven more reasons to come visit Blue Haven! It'll be hard to choose a favorite, but I dare you to try.

Love ya lattes,
Von Reklaw

***

"Don't worry, boy," I patted Scout on the head. He whined at me. "I'll be back and we'll go for a long walk." Those puppy eyes stared hard into me even after the front door was closed. I looked back to see Scout peeking at me through the window.

"Get a move on, Veronica! We don't want to be late." Gemma lifted her sunglasses and raised her brows to urge me to move faster.

"I'm coming, I'm coming."

I still couldn't believe I'd let Gemma convince me to exert this kind of energy before coffee. I picked up the pace and hit the unlock button so that Gemma could get into the car. I wasn't far behind. With the windows down and the music up, Gemma and I made our way down the driveway and over to the town of Bluewater.

I drove to Bluewater on a weekly basis for necessities. It's where the closest grocery store was when I needed to stock up on more than what was offered at the corner market in Blue Haven. The closest gas station was also in Bluewater. Gemma and I passed right by it on the way to Mindful Heart Yoga, where there was a parallel spot on the street waiting for us.

"I still can't believe you talked me into this," I said, pulling the key from the ignition.

"What?" Gemma always gave me the high-pitched voice when she wanted to seem innocent in a moment when she was guilty as hell. "I did no such thing," she winked before yanking the handle to open the door.

"Oh please! I'm going to look like a clown in there."

I ran behind the car to catch up with Gemma. She was way too wide awake this early in the morning. She was eager to get her yoga in, and I was counting down the minutes until I could hit up the coffee shop across the street.

When I pushed open the door to Mindful Heart, there was already a small group gathered in the room. Gemma and I checked in, grabbed a mat and stood in the back of the room to stake out the open spots. I leaned into Gemma so she could hear me whisper.

"Do you see her? I hope she looks like her profile picture," I said.

I didn't have to wait long to find out. Before Gemma could answer, two women entered the room and walked right past us. One of them had the same curly blonde hair as the photo Gemma had shown me. We looked at each other and nodded. That was definitely Linda Travis. Gemma went first. I followed closely behind her and we set up our yoga mats in the row behind Linda's. With less than ten minutes before class started, we had to move quickly.

"I'm so glad you convinced me to come to yoga," Gemma said loudly. "What a great way to keep my mind off the fact that we might have a... murderer in Blue Haven."

Linda Travis spun around immediately. She looked Gemma and I up and down. I've never felt so much judgement coming from a pair of eyes. I looked down at my stomach. The extra pounds I had gained this past winter were still covering my abs. I tugged at my shirt hoping to make it less noticeable.

"Do you two live in Blue Haven?" Linda asked.

"Oh, not me." Gemma waved her hands in front of her chest. "I'm visiting my good friend Veronica here."

The woman in downward dog next to Linda gasped as soon as Gemma said my name. She fell onto her knees and turned toward me. Her mouth was still wide open. Her finger pointed in my direction.

"You're her, aren't you? The one who found the body," she asked. I nodded. "Such a tragedy."

"It really was," I said. I pressed the bottoms of my feet together and leaned over them. I had to at least pretend I knew how to yoga. *How to yoga...* was yoga a verb? I shook my head and pulled myself back into the conversation. "Poor Wanda."

"Yes, poor Wanda. From what you've told me she was such a sweetheart," Gemma lied.

"Hah!" Linda let out a laugh, but immediately covered her mouth with the palm of her hand. The three of us looked at her. "I'm sorry. I must be hearing things. I thought you said that Wanda was a sweetheart."

"I did. Wasn't she?" Gemma asked. Her eyes were inquisitive. The way her bottom lip drooped made her look so innocent.

"Wanda Hemmings was many things, but a sweetheart was not one of them," Linda said. Honestly, if I knew who killed her, I'd probably shake their hand. I know that sounds terrible, but that woman was—she was awful."

I looked down at Linda's hands. They were clenched tight into fists as she went on about Wanda. Apparently, she'd been quite the controlling one when she was married to Jerry. That didn't surprise me. I used Linda's own words against her.

"Wow. I had no idea. I wonder if her husband is a suspect. I mean, the ex-husband is usually the first suspect."

Never mind that I knew Jerry had been out of town and his mother's assisted living home had already confirmed he was in Georgia at the time Wanda had been killed. I wanted to see Linda's reaction.

"Oh no! Not my Jerry. He couldn't hurt a fly," Linda said.

"Your Jerry?" Gemma was always good at acting surprised.

"Yes. We've been together for a while now, but way after Jerry and Wanda's divorce, of course."

"You poor thing." Gemma patted Linda's arm. "I bet you've also been tangled up in this mess. I couldn't imagine being the new girlfriend. Isn't that usually the second suspect in a case like this?"

I looked over at the woman next to Linda. Her jaw dropped again. She sunk back onto her mat and continued stretching. The instructor was now at the front of the room. Class was about to start.

"I guess," Linda answered Gemma's accusation. "Lucky for me I have a room full of women to vouch for where I was that morning."

Linda waved her arms and gestured to the room we were sitting in. I thought back to the day I'd found Wanda. I wondered if that was a day Linda had posted about yoga on her social media page. I made a mental note to check as the instructor called everyone's attention to the front of the room. I smiled at Linda one last time before she turned around and we all began to follow the teacher's instructions.

While everyone else closed their eyes and opened their hearts, I kept one eye open to make sure I followed the moves correctly. I wobbled a couple times in tree pose and was thankful when it was time to hit all fours, even if it was momentarily. It was the only time in class I felt grounded. In the middle of Vinyasa, I heard Gemma whisper my name. I crept a little closer to her.

"I have a plan," she whispered.

"For what?" I asked.

"We need to get to the computer after class."

I don't think our words were audible, but our whispers were enough to catch a few stares from the teacher. I moved a little closer to Gemma to try and keep it down.

"Are you crazy? We can't just walk behind the desk," I said.

"That's why I have a plan."

Gemma smiled up at the instructor who shot us another look. I moved back onto my mat and Gemma and I finished out our yoga in silence. The two of us sat for a long time on our mats once class was over pretending to sip our already-empty water bottles. Once it was just the two of us, Gemma let me in on her plan.

"I'm going to ask the teacher if she can help me with a couple of moves. That'll give you time to check the computer and see if Linda was in class that day."

My head fell into my hand. I was all about finding out who killed Wanda, but I didn't want to break the law doing it. I wanted to put someone else in jail, not get myself thrown in the slammer.

"Gemma, I cannot do that."

"Yes, you can and you're going to. Come on!"

Gemma grabbed my arm and lifted me up off the mat. I rolled mine up and threw it on the pile of used mats in the lobby while Gemma walked up to the instructor. My hands were shaking as I pulled my shoes from the cubby. Out of the corner of my eye I watched Gemma lead the teacher back into the room. I slid on my shoes and as slowly as I could, I tied the laces waiting for the last two women in the room to leave.

"Take your conversation outside," I whispered to myself.

You would've thought they'd heard me; within seconds they were heading out the door. It was my chance. I knew my window of opportunity was closing, so with weak knees, I hobbled over to the desk as fast as I could. The computer screen was still lit up with today's class list. I had no idea how to find previous classes. I grabbed the mouse and started clicking around until miraculously I found it! My heart was so heavy in my chest I thought it was going to knock me forward. I double-clicked on the date I needed. There had been a 7 am class that day. When the list of names was pulled up, I scrolled through it.

Linda wasn't lying. Her name was on the list. She'd checked in at six forty-five. That left only fifteen minutes for her to kill Wanda, clean herself up and drive over to Bluewater. This morning, with barely any traffic, it had taken me eight minutes to get to Bluewater from my house. It was probably an extra two or three from the boardwalk. There was no way Linda Travis could've killed Wanda. Another suspect checked off the list. I knew Declan was not going to be happy with how I'd obtained this information, but I had to tell him. I pulled out my phone and shot him a text.

Meet me at Peaches in an hour. Need to chat. —Veronica

I watched the three little dots dance beneath my text until his response came through.

Declan: See you in an hour.

I slipped out from behind the desk and back onto the bench right as Gemma reappeared. My lips quivered as I smiled in her direction. I gave her a subtle confirmation by brushing a thumbs up across my cheek and tried to look as innocent as possible until the two of us were free and clear and back on the streets of Bluewater.

CHAPTER TWELVE

Gemma and I were seated outside at Peaches Cafe a few minutes before Declan was set to arrive. My pulse had finally returned to normal after my brush with the law at the yoga studio. I wasn't quite sure that what I'd done was illegal, but if I'd gotten caught, I knew it would've been frowned upon.

"I have to admit, I really thought Linda would make a good killer," Gemma said. "I'm kind of disappointed to know she's innocent."

"Will you keep your voice down!" I shouted. The last thing I wanted was to bring anyone else in town in on the gossip.

"Oh, relax. No one can hear me. Where is this special agent of yours anyhow?" Gemma looked down at her watch. "I want to get some shopping in today."

"I'm sure he'll be here any minute," I said.

I reached down and wrapped my fingers around my glass full of orange juice. I was saving my second cup of coffee for Lattes All Day because I knew I'd need that free refill after a day of shopping with Gemma. I was in no hurry for Declan Grant to make his arrival so I could confess that I'd gone against his orders. I also knew that as soon as he sat down, Gemma would see all over my face that I was lying about him not being my type. Then I'd have to listen to her ideas on how she would get us together the rest of the time she was here.

I let the freshly-squeezed taste swish in my mouth before I drank it down. Then through a boisterous crowd of tourists, I saw a black polo shirt tucked into a pair of charcoal pants. I nearly tipped my glass, putting it back down on the table. Once Declan's eyes locked on mine, he waved. I stood to greet him.

"Hey there, good to see you again, Veronica," Grant said, raising his hand between us. That was the first time he'd called me by my first name. I wasn't sure if it meant anything, but it made me smile.

"Good to see you as well." I grabbed onto his hand and felt his other one rest on top of my shoulder. I could feel Gemma's eyes on us. I looked over at her trying to hide her sly smile with her napkin. "Declan, this is my friend Gemma. She's visiting from New York."

"Ah, the Big Apple. It's a pleasure."

"The pleasure is all mine," Gemma said, shaking Declan's hand.

Declan pulled out the only empty chair at the table and lowered himself onto it. Our waitress came to take his order and once she'd left, we got down to business.

"So, you wanted to chat?" Declan was hesitant to say any more with Gemma around, but he was going to find out anyway, so I let it all spill out.

"Uh... yes... the case." I closed my eyes and took a deep breath to ready myself. "Gemma and I went to yoga this morning and coincidentally ran into Linda Travis."

"Coincidentally?" Declan's brows furrowed and he took his eyes off me only to thank the waitress for his coffee. "Go on."

"Well, it turns out the day Wanda was killed, she was at a yoga class. She checked in only fifteen minutes after your team called the time of death," I said.

Declan lifted the coral-colored ceramic mug to his lips. He took a long sip and I could tell by the wrinkles that appeared on his forehead that he was thinking very hard about what I had said. If he could read between the lines, which was obviously part of his job, I would need to field some questions.

"And how do you know Linda was at yoga?" Declan asked.

"She told me," I said.

"Veronica, I told you that you have to be careful about how you go about handling this case. Not only is it dangerous for you, but one wrong move could really jeopardize this case."

"I know, I know, but I..."

Gemma didn't let me finish. "Oh, I was very convincing. She had no idea we were digging for clues, trust me."

"I take it Veronica here filled you in." Declan took another sip of his coffee.

"Only on the things the town has already been gossiping about. Veronica is very professional, Gemma winked. "I was the one who forced her to check the studio computer for the..."

Declan pulled the mug from his mouth and turned his head as coffee flew from his lips. "To do *what?*"

I shot Gemma a wide-eyed look. I'd planned to ease into that confession, not rip off the band aid. I clasped my hands into my lap and prepared to tell the rest of the story.

"So, I may have checked the roster on the studio computer for that day while the teacher was preoccupied," I confessed.

Declan rubbed his hand over the back of his neck. I could see the beads of sweat forming on his forehead. I smiled at him with my "I was just trying to help" smile in hopes he would cut me a break. He did.

"Okay, listen, though I appreciate your enthusiasm, and the information, I'm only going to say this one more time—you have to be careful. There's a real killer out there and if they get wind of you sneaking around looking for answers, you could be put in some serious danger." I nodded. "From now on, no investigating without me. Got it?"

Gemma and I looked at each other and then back at Declan. We both agreed, but I had to admit it was kind of satisfying to know that I delivered information that could help the case. Before Declan went off to continue his own legitimate investigation, he pulled out his notepad and scribbled down a few lines. He took one last sip of his coffee, shook both my and Gemma's hands, and headed on his way. Once he was out of earshot, Gemma slapped the bare part of my shoulder.

"Ow! What was that for?" I asked.

"He is so your type," she said. "And you so *looooove* him."

"I do not!" I shrieked as the waitress slid the check on the table.

"Oh, you so do. I don't blame you. That tanned skin and the way he filled out the sleeves of his shirt... oh my." Gemma started waving her hand in front of her face.

"Yeah, yeah. Just for that, you can get the check." I slid the check in front of her.

"Fine." Gemma swiped the check and threw a few bills on top of it. "Deny it all you want, for now. After we're done shopping, though, and we're deep into our nightly mud mask, we're talking about this."

I shook my head and threw my purse over my shoulder. I could read Gemma like a book, but I guess I could say the same about her. As much as I wanted to deny my growing attraction to Declan Grant, the more I was around him, the harder I was unable to ignore the way my heart raced when he looked in my direction.

CHAPTER THIRTEEN

The Best Blueberry Waffles in Blue Haven Can Be Found Where?

I'm still hungover from the excess of blueberry waffles I fancied at Peaches Cafe. Yup, you read that right! Peaches Cafe has the best blueberry waffles. Oh, the irony. The fluffiness of each bite was like digging my fork right into Cloud 9. I have to restrain myself every morning not to head right back down to Peaches so I don't end up like the blueberry girl in that classic candy-loving movie we all adore.

The pecan maple syrup that accompanies the blueberry waffles makes for an excellent flavor burst. And every breakfast dish comes with a side of fresh-baked peach compote. Don't skip this stop on your next visit to Blue Haven. Your taste buds will thank me.

Love ya lattes,
Von Reklaw

***

Gemma begged me to take her to Peaches Cafe so she could see if Suzy Atwater's blueberry waffles were as amazing as Von Reklaw had said they were. She agreed after three bites and left the rest for the seagulls. I, on the other hand, never left a bite on my plate. I regretted it as we shopped on the boardwalk. My stomach felt like I'd swallowed a bowling ball, but I tried not to let it get in the way of the fun Gemma was having.

"What do you think of this?" Gemma asked. She popped out from behind the curtain at the Blue Haven thrift store. With her arms opened wide, she twirled in a flowy, yellow beach coverup. "It's the only thing I forgot to pack in my suitcase and I am giving myself a beach day while I'm here."

"I like it," I said.

"Good, because I was getting it anyway."

I didn't doubt it. Gemma was as Ms. Independent as they came. She'd never had a long-term boyfriend. She liked being single and focusing on her journalism career. That was a good thing, since being a journalist in New York was incredibly hard. Dozens of others were always vying for the same position you were hoping to get. It was one of the reasons I hadn't felt like I was giving anything up when I'd moved to Blue Haven. Starting my own blog here had had much less competition and the mystery of it all had been pretty fun.

Once Gemma was dressed back in the clothes she'd pulled from her suitcase that morning and her coverup was paid for, we moved back out onto the boardwalk and off to the next store that might catch her eye. We had a few hours before my dog walking duties would kick in. I knew Gemma would take up every bit of that time.

"Oh, buy one get one free!" Gemma pointed at the A-Frame standing outside Scented Wicks Candle shop. The neon cursive letters with little hearts made the sale even more irresistible to Gemma. "I love candles! Let's go!"

I felt a twinge at my shoulder as Gemma yanked my arm and pulled me in. I'd only been in Scented Wicks once or twice since I'd been in Blue Haven. I'd bought one for my mom when her birthday had come and one as a housewarming gift to myself when I was fully unpacked in the farmhouse. It was on its last flicker. Maybe I too would take advantage of the buy one get one.

Mae met us at the entrance. Her deep red lipstick was a stark contrast to the paleness of her skin. The roots of her naturally gray hair that had been peeking through when I'd seen her at the market had this time been covered with a jet black dye.

"Hello, ladies! Veronica, how are you?" Mae's hand fell onto my shoulder and the same dread-filled look everyone else gave me once they realized I was the girl who'd found the body came across her face.

"I'm doing much better now, thank you. How about you? You saw the dreadful scene as well," I said.

"Yes, that is true. I'm hanging in there. I do hope they catch the perp soon," Mae said. "I heard Suzy Atwater and Farmer Don are on the list of suspects. Neither of them would surprise me."

News traveled fast in small towns. Those were the lead suspects on the list. Farmer Don had seemed more likely to overtake Wanda than Suzy Atwater, but the fact that Suzy was only a few doors down that morning gave her a definite opportunity. I didn't play into Mae's accusations. I wanted to be careful, like with all nosy residents, to not let on that I knew more than I should.

"They sure seem to be the talk of the town right now," I said.

"Anyway, I don't want to spoil your day with this talk. I'm glad to see you're doing well," Mae said. "Take a look around the shop and let me know if you have any questions."

"We will, Mae. Thank you," I said.

Gemma and I crowded around the table of beach-scented candles. We both started pulling off the tops and sticking our noses over the wax. Gemma would tip each one in her hand to me for approval.

"This beechwood one smells amazing. Kind of like the cologne that handsome detective was wearing this morning," Gemma joked. I looked over at her and glared through narrowed eyes. She shrugged. "What? It does. Speaking of detective," Gemma's voice turned into a whisper, "I wonder who he'll be talking to next."

"I'm almost certain that whoever it is, he probably isn't going to tell me. I failed in the sleuthing department. Not only did I go against his orders, but I spilled all my secrets to you. If I worked with him, he would've fired me by now," I said, picking up the seaside coconut candle.

"No way! Without you, he'd probably still think Little Miss Yoga was a suspect. If I had to put my money on it, I would say that you are going to figure out who killed the old lady before he does."

"Maybe," I said. "It would be kind of cool. It would also help me sleep better at night."

"You're not kidding."

"Seaside coconut is my favorite!"

I wasn't prepared for the voice behind me. I jumped back and the candle slipped from my grasp. I felt as if I'd been transported to one of those dream sequences you see in a movie. There it was, a fragile, white candle being pulled to the floor thanks to that little thing we call gravity. I felt my jaw fall with it as I bent down and reached out my hands. I held my breath as the candle sailed closer to the floor. I pulled my hands out further and when I felt the cold glass against my skin, I let out a heavy sigh.

"Mae, you scared me," I said. I gripped the candle tightly and stood up to meet her.

"I'm sorry, hun! I didn't mean to. You have great taste. I sold out of my first shipment already. Those came in yesterday."

"Oh, lucky me that I came in today," I said.

Gemma looked over at me. I was still clutching the candle to my chest. She laughed and then moved away from the beach scents and picked up a caramel apple-scented candle. Mae slithered away to another customer. I couldn't bring myself to let go of the seaside coconut candle, so I tucked it under my arm and followed Gemma to the next table. I didn't realize how much I would enjoy having Gemma here in Blue Haven. I'd gotten to know a lot of residents here, but there was something about an old friend in a new town that made today a little brighter.

CHAPTER FOURTEEN

Gemma wasn't going to leave Blue Haven without a relaxation day down at the beach. By ten o'clock the next morning our beach towels were sprawled out on the sand, and a blue and white striped umbrella covered us. Well, it covered me. Gemma was lathered in tanning oil from head to toe and was basking in the cloudless sky. My Irish skin wouldn't survive that. I had my SPF 50 on and I was taking full advantage of my rented protection.

"This totally beats the faux rooftop tanning deck I created outside the window of my apartment," Gemma said.

"What are you talking about? I loved that faux tanning deck," I said.

For anyone who doesn't know about life in New York City, I'm talking about the tiny box of outdoor space that existed outside the kitchen window. We had to crawl out the window to access it. The sun hit that side of the building for only about an hour or two a day. Gemma planned her weekends around that sun in the summertime. She'd wake me up early to run errands so that by the time the sun was staring down on that part of the apartment she was home and ready.

"It does come in handy when I'm too lazy to walk eight flights of stairs for fresh air," Gemma laughed. "It misses you!"

I looked over at Gemma. I could see the wink through her sunglasses. It was no secret that one of Gemma's missions in coming here was to convince me to go back to New York. I wasn't ready yet to talk about all the things besides Gemma that were trying to pull me back up north. There was a laundry list of reasons to stay far away.

"I have to tell you, those eight flights of stairs are what I miss the least," I laughed. "Well, maybe the second least. I miss not running into Jonathan on every corner of the city. I swear, I saw him more after we broke up than when we were dating."

"Ugh, that reminds me. I saw him last week at the bodega. Him and that girl of his. What's her name? Aubrey... Audrey..."

"Audrianna," I finished her sentence.

"Right. I ducked down the chip aisle when I saw them come in. I tiptoed backward but lost them at the popcorn. Then, I turned around and *BAM!* I ran right into them."

"No way! Did he say anything to you?"

I moved off my beach chair and slid through the sand closer to where Gemma was lying. I didn't want to miss a word of this story and the group of guys that sat down a few feet from us were now blaring their rock music from their portable speaker.

"He tried to play it off like he didn't recognize me. He apologized and started to walk away, but you know I wasn't going to let him get off that easy. I said his name and told him how lovely it was to see him again. I asked him to introduce me to his friend. When she corrected me with the word 'girlfriend,' I kindly reminded her how I was your old roommate and went on to talk about your fabulous new life. She dragged him away before I could finish."

I'd always wished I was courageous like Gemma. I'd found out about Jonathan's other girlfriend while planning a special night out for his birthday. I was leaving the balloon shop near Washington Square Park; I'd put an order in the night before. The shop was right around the corner from his apartment. I was going to grab them, sneak into his apartment while he was at a rehearsal for his play, and decorate. We'd been dating long enough that I had a key.

It was a nice night, so I'd decided to take a walk in the park before hopping on the 6th train home. He was supposed to be rehearsing that night, or that's what he'd told me anyway. I spotted him sitting on a bench in the park, and Audrianna was sitting next to him. She was his co-star, so I gave him the benefit of the doubt until he leaned in and started kissing her. I walked up and didn't say a word. He turned pale when he saw me and I dumped the rest of my water bottle in his face.

I cried every step to the 6th train. I managed to hold it in while I was squished in-between the rush hour crowd. I ran up all eight flights of stairs to tell Gemma. I never wanted to see Jonathan again after that. Gemma returned his apartment key and the few things he had hanging around our apartment. He traded those for the rest of my things, but shortly after that, I saw him everywhere. That's why I took my Nana's farmhouse as a sign that it was time to get out of the city. I can't believe Audrianna stayed with him after that. I was thankful it was her and not me.

"I feel sorry for her. I can't imagine he hasn't found someone else by now," I said.

"He's an actor," Gemma said. "He's good at telling stories. I'm sure he somehow convinced her you were crazy."

"I can't believe this is the first I'm hearing about this," I said.

"Honestly, I didn't want to rain on your parade. I know he's a sensitive subject, but then I got here and I saw how amazing you're doing and thought you could use a laugh."

Our conversation was interrupted when a gust of sand flew into Gemma's face. She screamed and I turned to find a football lying at my feet. A pair of muscled calves were running toward us. I closed my eyes to escape the bits of sand that were still flying in our direction.

"I'm sorry about that."

I looked up to find a bare-chested guy sweeping the football into his arms. His black hair was long enough that the wind had caught it and swept it across his face. I braced myself for the wrath I was expecting to come from

Gemma. The apologetic look in his eyes made me feel sorry for what he was about to experience.

"That's okay," Gemma blushed. "Just don't let it happen again or I'll make you buy me a drink."

"Well, I don't know about a drink, but the ice cream cart is coming this way," he said.

"Oh no, I've had enough calories for the day. On your way," Gemma shooed him.

He tossed the football between his hands a couple more times before he turned and headed back to the rest of his group. I looked over and shook my head. Gemma shrugged and laid her head back down on her towel.

"I wish I could be more like you," I said.

"No, you don't," she said. "You're sweet and innocent and I love that about you. You don't need guys like that. They are only good for one-night stands. Girls like you deserve guys like the handsome detective." I started to object. "Don't you dare! I saw the way you looked at him and how he placed his hand on your shoulder. He definitely lingered."

"Lingered?"

"Yes! He took advantage of that moment to be close to you. He lingered. He likes you," Gemma insisted.

"He's trying to solve a murder case and I happen to be the girl who found the body," I said.

"Nope, it's more than that. I have good instincts when it comes to these things."

I rested my hand on my chin and raised my eyebrows at her. I wondered if she'd conveniently forgotten how I'd ended up dating Jonathan in the first place. She'd made me wait outside the back door of the theater after the show we'd gone to see was finished. We'd waited about an hour. When Jonathan had walked out she'd slid him a business card pretending she wanted to interview him. What she didn't tell me was she'd written about my desperation on the back of it. He'd showed me on our third date what it said.

My friend thinks you're cute. You should buy her a drink. My name and number were written underneath.

"Okay, okay," Gemma admitted, "so I messed up one time. I'm right about this one though. I know I am."

"We'll see about that," I said.

I sat back in my beach chair and closed my eyes. I tried to forget about the possibility that Gemma could be right. I think I wanted it to be true more than it was, but I couldn't help but smile when his face filled my thoughts, as I listened to the rush of the waves meeting the sand at my feet.

CHAPTER FIFTEEN

Beach Bums Flock to Blue Haven for This Unique Offering

A day of relaxation in Blue Haven is just that; once you pop up your beach chair, you won't need to move a muscle in order to enjoy some of the deliciousness this town has to offer. Eddie's Bagel Bike rides the beaches until 2 pm. All bagels are made by Eddie himself. Take a peek into the bike's front basket and you'll find over a dozen flavors of cream cheese. Remember to wait thirty minutes after indulging before you hit the ocean.

An afternoon swim is sure to work up an appetite. Thankfully, Mike's ice cream cart is open seven days a week from noon until sunset. Mike's cart features everything from ice cream sandwiches and single scoop flavors to Italian ice pops. It's the perfect snack before you fold up your towel for the day and enjoy a casual dinner on the boardwalk.

It's amazing to think that all of Blue Haven's culinary choices are individually owned and operated by our own residents. Come support the local scene here and enjoy the pristine beaches while you're at it.

Love ya lattes,
Von Reklaw

***

The sun had officially set on Blue Haven after a long day at the beach. Gemma and I had already been home for a couple of hours. Our hair was still damp from the long showers we'd both taken to get the sand out of, well, everywhere. Scout was nestled up next to me on the couch when the alarm on my phone went off.

It was time for dog duty. I slid my feet to the floor and pushed my now sunburned self off of the couch. Scout followed. His tail of course was wagging. I think that by now he's associated my phone alarm with long walks with his friends.

"You can stay here if you want," I said. Gemma looked comfortable in the plump chair across from me.

"No, that's okay. I am loving these nightly walks in the fresh coastal air. Let me grab my hat."

I got Scout ready while Gemma ran upstairs, and once she came down, we were on our way, Scout in the lead. His body wiggled the whole way to Halo's house. She was a mini Goldendoodle. Her owner, Jack, was a bartender. He worked a few towns over where there were actually bars and the town stayed open until about two in the morning. Here in Blue Haven everything shut down by ten. Everything except my dog walking business, that is.

When I'd started dog walking, I'd tried to set a schedule. No earlier than seven in the morning and no later than eight in the evening, but later I'd learned to work when the business needed me, and a couple of nights a week that meant ten.

Halo's tail was going crazy when I flicked on the light. Her front paws were balancing on the black wire of her cage, waiting for me to let her out. When I did she ran through my legs and nuzzled herself underneath Scout.

"Aw, she loves him," Gemma said.

"Haha, I know. I think it's safe to say that Halo is Scout's favorite."

I slid Halo's purple harness on and clipped her leash as fast as I could so she didn't run out the door without me. The night sky was incredibly bright, and the humidity from early in the day had pretty much disappeared. It was a gorgeous night for a walk on the beach and the much-needed girl talk I had missed since I'd left New York.

"So, have you given any more thought to my offer?" Gemma asked. "I know a startup is risky, but I think you'd be good at it."

I'd known this topic was going to come up eventually. I was surprised she hadn't brought it up on the beach that morning. My room hadn't even been rented in New York yet when Gemma had started begging me to come back, within a month of my leaving. There was a new culinary magazine that had launched and they were looking for a food critic to take on the scene in the city. Gemma had taken a job with them and showed them what little I had created of the Kaffeinated Kitchen blog back then. They'd loved it so much they hadn't even wanted to interview me. They had wanted to offer me the job and even pay to relocate me back to the city.

I'd worked for more than a decade in New York City for the chance at an opportunity like this. It figured it would come as soon as I left. The offer was tempting, and it would certainly pay more than my blog and dog walking were currently making, combined.

"I've sort of put it on the back burner since Wanda died, but I'm still thinking about it," I said.

"You could move in with me again. I'll kick my newest roommate out. I hate how she leaves her dishes in the sink, anyway," Gemma said. "The editor said he'd give you free rein of the restaurants. It's basically your dream job on a silver platter."

I sighed. I knew she was right. It would be stupid of me to pass it up, but there was something about my life in Blue Haven that was keeping me from pulling the trigger. I loved living in the farmhouse. Scout loved having a yard and not having to go to the bathroom on the concrete because we couldn't find a patch of grass fast enough.

Blue Haven was laid back. I know New York City had Central Park, but there was something magical about spending my free time reading on the beach while the water drifted over my toes. This was also the first year of my entire life that I hadn't had to trudge through slush and snow in the winter to get somewhere. And I thought my hours of sleep must have increased every night without the sirens and car horns seeping through my window at all hours. I loved New York, but maybe that part of my life was over now. Maybe. I was telling Gemma the truth: I was still thinking about it.

"I kind of like it down here," I said. "I know it's not as glamorous or as exciting, but it's growing on me."

By that time Gemma and I were trudging through the soft sand on the beach, past the now closed ice cream cart Gemma had almost got a taste of earlier. Scout and Halo were jumping at each other and the only sound aside from their panting was the whisper of the night waves.

"I get it," Gemma said. "It's cute down here, but they aren't going to wait forever. I can probably stall them for another week or two."

"Thanks," I said.

Gemma threw her arm around my shoulder and pulled me in while we walked down the beach. We walked quite a ways until Halo had no energy left. Her little tongue was hanging out and she was begging Gemma to pick her up. When Gemma did so, Halo rested underneath her chin until we were back on the boardwalk.

"Okay, little one, you still have to go potty," I said.

Gemma lowered her to the ground. Halo hopped on the grass and spun in a few circles before she found the right spot.

"That's all you," Gemma said, handing me Halo's leash.

I laughed and traded her Scout's leash. She kept walking while I waited for Halo to finish and do my duty of being a responsible dog walker. The closest garbage bin was behind us, so I let Gemma keep walking with Scout, who had momentarily locked eyes with a bird and tried to stake his territory with a few deep barks. As soon as I had thrown the bag in the garbage, I heard a scream from the other end of the boardwalk. I spun around. Gemma was the only one there. She screamed again and I picked up Halo and ran towards her.

"What? What happened?" I yelled.

"Someone is in that alley! They tried to attack me."

It must have been the adrenaline because, without hesitation, I tossed Halo into Gemma's arms and ran toward the alley. It was dark, but a faint light from the top of the brick building gave off just enough brightness to cast a shadow. I could see someone push through the fence and take off down the other alley to the next street over.

"Hey!" I yelled.

I wasn't brave enough to continue down the alley, but I did run back out to the boardwalk and around the corner to see if I could catch them on the other side of the street. I wasn't fast enough; the figure disappeared into the dark. My breath was heavy as I stared at the empty street. What the hell had just happened?

I was still trying to catch my breath when I heard footsteps beside me. I jumped back and screamed.

"Woah, it's just me!" Gemma said. "Do you see anyone down there?" I shook my head. "They had something in their hand. It looked like a baseball bat."

"*Seriously?*" I asked.

"Yeah! When I walked into the opening, they ran at me. They stopped when I screamed and then turned and ran."

"I'm calling Declan. This is insane," I said.

My hands were shaking so badly that I could barely grip the phone in my purse to pull it out. It took three times for the phone to recognize my face because I couldn't hold it still. Once it did, I spoke the words, *call Declan Grant,* and waited for an answer.

"Special Agent Grant," the deep voice on the other end came through.

"Declan, it's Veronica. My friend Gemma almost got attacked in the alley next to Wanda's Cafe. The person ran. They're gone now."

"I'm going to send a unit over there to check things out. You two go home. Send me your address and I'll meet you there as soon as I can."

"Okay, thank you," I said. I hung up and looked over at Gemma. "Are you alright? Did you see the person at all?"

"Not really. It was dark in the alley," Gemma said.

I could tell she was still shaken up. Her shoulders were tense and Halo was squirming in her tight grasp. Scout jumped up on me and I petted his fluffy ears. His whine was high-pitched and I knew he could feel the fear between Gemma and me.

"Come on, let's get Halo back. The detective is meeting us at my house."

"Hopefully we make it back there alive," Gemma whispered.

The two of us started walking as fast as we could away from the boardwalk. I led the way with the flashlight on my phone and Gemma stayed close behind me. Scout had forgotten about what had happened halfway to Halo's and began galloping in front of me until we got into the house. I set Halo back in her cage and Gemma stood watch by the front door in case anyone was following us. I flicked off the light, closed the door, and the two of us, along with Scout, walked wide-eyed all the way home.

CHAPTER SIXTEEN

Even though we knew Declan was going to be showing up soon, the knock on the door had Gemma and I both shaking. I reached over for the iron poker next to the living room fireplace and gripped it tight in front of my chest. Gemma stayed in the living room, peering with her head around the wall, watching me as I tiptoed to the front door. I pulled the curtain back far enough to be able to let out a sigh of relief. Declan was standing out on the porch. I lowered the poker and unlocked the door to let him in.

"Hi," I said.

"Are you ladies alright?" Declan asked once he was inside.

"I think so. I didn't really see anything. Poor Gemma was the one they came after," I said.

I closed the front door and Declan let himself into the living room, where Gemma was waiting. He sat on my grandmother's favorite blue-upholstered chair and Gemma and I sat across from him on the white microfiber couch I'd bought after I'd moved in. With his notebook and pen already in hand, he began to ask questions.

"Do you know if the person who tried to attack you was a man or woman?" Declan asked. Gemma shook her head. "Can you describe them in any way? Hair, facial features, height?"

"It was dark," Gemma said "I didn't get a good look at them, but I would say they were shorter than I was. Maybe 5'5". They were a little stocky. From their silhouette, I'd say they carried a lot of weight in their middle section."

"And you said they had a baseball bat?" Declan asked. Gemma nodded again. "Did they say anything to you?"

For most of the questioning, Gemma's hands had fidgeted in her lap. Her facial expressions were serious yet stoic, but when Declan asked if the person said anything, her demeanor changed. Her brows lifted and she turned pale.

"They did!" Gemma's voice rose. "I didn't remember until now, but they did! When I first saw them, I was walking close to the buildings where it was dark. Then, I noticed them, screamed, and jumped back closer to the street lamp. As soon as I did that, they stopped. They said, 'You're not her.'"

"'You're not her?'" Declan repeated.

"Yeah, then they retreated into the alley. That's when Veronica showed up and they ran away."

"Oh my gosh," I said.

I threw my hand over my mouth and tried to swallow the lump that had appeared in my throat. I'd been walking that boardwalk for months. Very rarely was there anyone on it in the evenings when I was out. Granted, I'd never walked there past maybe eight o'clock, since I was usually by myself, but I couldn't imagine there would be many other people out at a later time. That person had to have heard us coming. Gemma and I had been laughing and chatting and Scout had barked at a bird only seconds before.

"Do you think I'm... her?" The words fumbled out of my mouth. "If I hadn't stopped for Halo, I would've been right there with you. Do you think it was Farmer Don?" I looked over at Declan.

"He is short and pudgy, but how would he have known you were going to be on the boardwalk that night? He lives pretty far out to run into by coincidence," Declan said.

"True," I said.

"Is it possible they followed you onto the boardwalk?" Declan asked.

"I guess anything is possible, but Scout usually notices those kinds of things," I said. "And we were on the beach for quite a long time. How would they know when or which way we'd walk back?"

"They had to have seen you then once you got to the boardwalk. Perhaps they live nearby." Declan made a few more notes.

"I didn't hear any cars once they ran off," Gemma said. "No engine or squealing of tires. I mean, where else could they have gone?"

"I have a unit over there now. I'll see if the cameras picked anything up. Being that this town hasn't seen any real big crimes, the security cameras are limited," Declan said. "No business has them inside or out. There's none in front of Wanda's Cafe. I checked the day she was killed."

"Great." Gemma sighed heavily and let her chin fall into her hands.

"I have to admit, it's hard to think this incident isn't related to the detective work you've been doing," Declan said.

His stare burned into me with that statement. I wanted to defend myself, but I couldn't help but agree. Especially after the snooping at the yoga studio. Declan was right; I should've been more careful. Now I was in over my head and someone knew it.

"From now on, if you find any more information, Veronica, I need you to tell me first. Don't go off and try to handle it on your own. Promise me," Declan said.

"I promise."

"And in the meantime, be more vigilant. If you see anyone following you, don't go home. Head straight to the station."

I promised Declan that I would follow his orders from that day forward. I wanted to find out who killed Wanda, but I didn't want it to be at the expense of my own life. Not to mention I was now putting Gemma in the middle of all of it. I would never forgive myself if something happened to her.

I thanked Declan for coming over so late and was sure to double lock the door behind him. Besides scaring the crap out of us, tonight had confirmed one thing for Gemma and me: whoever had killed Wanda was going to stop at nothing to get away with it, even if that meant they had to keep killing to do so.

CHAPTER SEVENTEEN

The Quiche on the Beach Bake Off... Will They or Won't They?

I opened my email this morning while enjoying a delectable cherry cheesecake donut from Blue Haven Donuts. I was shocked at both the email and at how amazing the maple glaze paired with the cherry flavor of the donut. I didn't think it could get much better than the red velvet long john they'd served in February, but I was wrong.

If you're heading to Blue Haven this month, add this donut to your list of beach snacks. It may not make it to the beach once it's in your hands, but at least it'll keep you satisfied while you're basking in the sun on our amazing beaches.

Back to the big topic at hand: it seems that Mayor Allen is ready to speak on the status of the Quiche on the Beach Bake Off. There has been a lot of discussion between the town and the event committee and with only days until the bake off is set to begin, a decision has been made.

The meeting starts at 4 pm sharp. Get there early if you want a seat. I don't know a single resident who hasn't been waiting for this announcement.

Love ya lattes,
Von Reklaw

***

I tried to lock eyes with as many people as I could the night after the almost-attack. I'd dragged Gemma to the town meeting. We were set to discuss the ultimate fate of the Quiche on the Beach Bake Off. The whole town was crowded into the town hall and Mayor Allen was hitting his gavel onto the podium.

"Good evening everyone. Thank you for coming tonight," he said. "We have a couple of very important matters on the agenda, the first being our beloved annual bake off. I know there has been some talk that we weren't going forward with the event, but after much consideration we have decided that we will be hosting the bake off this year."

There was a brief silence before the crowd broke out into applause. Suzy Atwater, who was also standing near the front of the room, stepped in front of the podium. She waited for the crowd to settle down before she added onto Mayor Allen's comments.

"As someone who has been a part of this event for some time now, I'm happy to share that this year we will be dedicating the bake off to our dear friend Wanda."

Suzy stopped for effect. She wiped her eyes and sniffled into the microphone. I looked around to see if anyone was buying it. They weren't. I saw some roll their eyes and others laugh into their hands. I did a mixture of both, but we all let her carry on.

"We all know how much Wanda loved the bake off and the pride that she took in perfecting her recipe every year. As sad as I am that she won't be with us this year, I know that she will want us to go on and celebrate in her honor."

Suzy didn't get quite the applause that the mayor had, but the fact that the attention was on her for a full five minutes was enough for her. She stepped back and combed her hands through her hair as the mayor stepped up again to announce the next topic on the agenda.

"Blue Haven, I know there are a lot of questions about Wanda, so I wanted to bring in a couple of people to help answer them for you. Please welcome Blue Haven's police chief, Richard Hart, and Special Agent Declan Grant."

The door in front of the hall popped open and in walked Declan and Richard Hart. Declan stepped up to the podium first. He fielded most of the questions.

"Do you have any suspects?" one person asked.

"We have identified a few persons of interest," Declan answered.

"Is there reason to be worried they may strike again?"

"We are doing everything we can to close this case as quickly as possible. Right now, we ask that everyone be vigilant and report any suspicious activity to the police. If anyone has any information, we also ask you to come forward as even the smallest details can be helpful."

Declan took a few more questions. As he finished, I felt something jab hard into my side. I reached over and felt Gemma's elbow. I didn't look over at first. We were in close quarters so I thought it had been an accident. After the second time, I jerked my head and shot her a look. She leaned closer to me.

"I see that smile on your face," she whispered.

"What smile?"

"The one that appeared when the detective walked in."

"Will you stop?" I could feel the heat on my face.

I was blushing because I knew she was right. I didn't think I had made it obvious for anyone else to notice, but this was Gemma we were talking about. She noticed everything when it came to romance. Not that there was anything romantic going on between Declan and me. I simply couldn't help but notice how manly he looked standing up there. He answered every question so confidently, staring directly at the person with those bright, inquisitive, eyes.

"You shouldn't be embarrassed," Gemma assured me. "It's not like he's married or anything." She paused for a moment. "Right?"

I shook my head. "No, he's not married."

"Girlfriend?" Gemma asked.

I shrugged and thought back to our conversation at the Farmers Market. I knew he wanted a wife, but I wasn't sure if he were actively looking. Not that I had a desire to fill that role. I had only known him for a few weeks. We had a few things in common, like our love for croissants and coffee, but other than that I didn't know where he lived or what he liked to do outside of work. I did know that he seemed caring and compassionate and genuinely worried for my safety.

"I guess we have some other kind of detective work to do then, don't we," Gemma winked.

I slapped her upper arm and tried to refocus my attention back to the front of the room. Declan was no longer at the podium. Mayor Allen had traded places with him.

"Thank you again, everyone, for coming. As the detective said, please keep an eye out and report anything suspicious you may see. I know we're all ready to get Blue Haven back to the safe, worry-free town we've always been. This meeting is adjourned."

I didn't think the gavel was necessary, but Mayor Allen used it to hit the podium one last time. Gemma and I waited for our row to clear and headed out the back door with the rest of the crowd.

We made it out of the town hall and were about to get into my car when I heard my name being called. My hand froze on the door handle and I turned around. It took a minute for the crowd to clear. Declan was jogging toward me.

"Hey, Veronica," he said. "Do you two have time this evening to stop by the station? I have a few more questions I'd like to ask, based on some things the team found last night."

I looked over at Gemma. She nodded.

"Yeah, sure. I have to walk a couple of dogs right now, but we can head over after if that works for you."

"That's great. I'll see you in a bit. Be careful," Declan said.

He turned back to the crowd and Gemma and I got into my car. It would be a quick walk and a stop to check on Scout before we ended up at the station where Declan was waiting for us.

"How can I help you?" A brown-haired woman with her hair in a bun was sitting at the front desk of the station.

"We're here to see Dec—" I paused, thinking it would be more professional to not use Declan's first name. "Special Agent Grant. He's expecting us."

"Name?"

"Veronica Walker," I said.

The woman picked up the phone, pressed a few buttons and I could hear a muffled answer on the other end. She said my name, nodded, and hung the phone back up. She looked back down at the pile of paperwork in front of her.

"Down the hall, second door on the right," she said.

Gemma and I stood there for another few seconds before I realized she was talking to me. We started down the hallway past the row of window walls and empty offices before we found Declan with his head buried in his notebook. I knocked softly on his open door.

"Veronica, come in." Declan stood up as the two of us entered. "Thank you for coming over on such short notice. The officers found something last night around the area you said you were attacked. I wanted to see if you recognized it."

Declan pulled a plastic bag from his desk drawer and set it in front of us. Inside was a tiny bottle of perfume. The purple glass was in the shape of a heart.

"It doesn't look familiar," I said.

"That is some expensive perfume though. Does that mean the perp is a woman?" Gemma asked.

"Well, we don't know that for sure, but are you familiar with the brand?" Declan asked Gemma.

"Oh, yeah! Everyone in New York loves it. It's the newest from Felicia Mac." Declan and I both gave Gemma a blank stare. "You don't know Felicia Mac? She's like the hottest new movie star. They did a special release maybe two months ago in New York. It's called Lavender Delight."

"Wait! Did you say lavender?" I asked. Gemma nodded. My jaw dropped and I fell back into my chair.

"What's wrong?" Declan asked.

"When I first walked into Wanda's I... before I found her body, there was a very strong scent of lavender that filled the room. I think whoever killed Wanda was wearing that perfume, but if it's not Suzy or Linda, who else could it be?"

"I wish we knew. We did pick up a print from the bottle and guess what? It was a match to the one found on the frying pan."

"That's great news!" Gemma yelled.

"Yes and no," Declan said. "I would say this confirms that whoever killed Wanda knows you've been digging around. This attack doesn't seem random, but we have the same problem. This fingerprint isn't in the database. Therefore we're back to square one."

Declan bent down and opened the bottom drawer of the filing cabinet. He ruffled through a few folders before coming to the one with Wanda's name on it and tossing it down on his desk. He flipped open the folder and started turning pages. Gemma and I waited to see if he found anything. About halfway through, Declan pulled out a notecard in a plastic bag and set it on his desk while continuing to comb through papers.

"What's that?" I asked.

"Oh, that's the recipe card that we found underneath Wanda. It must have been her quiche recipe for this year that she was working on."

"May I?" I asked.

"Go for it."

I picked the bag up to take a closer look. Pie crust, eggs, heavy cream... this was certainly a quiche recipe, but that wasn't Wanda's handwriting. I collected a questionnaire for each of my dog walking clients. It asked simple questions like emergency contact, allergies, and special requests. I screenshot them and save them in the favorites folder of my phone so I always have them with me. I unzipped my purse, pulled my phone out, and opened it to that folder. I scrolled through until I found Wanda's file. Gemma leaned in.

"What are you doing?" Gemma asked.

"If this was Wanda's quiche recipe, she didn't write it." I tipped my phone toward Gemma. "Look. Wanda's handwriting is rigid. She wrote all in capital letters. The words on this note card are fancy. Look at all these squiggles and these little hearts."

"Oh yeah, you're right." Gemma took the notecard from my hand. "This looks completely different than Wanda's handwriting."

Gemma pulled the notecard closer to her face, then back down to her lap. She scrunched her nose and rubbed her fingers over her chin. Declan set the papers down and reached out to take a look at the photo on my phone.

"This is an interesting discovery," he said.

"It doesn't make sense," I said. "Wanda never let anyone see her recipes. It's weird that someone else would write it down for her." I looked down at my watch. It was a quarter past seven. Dotty's bakery closed at eight. "Shoot! We have to go."

I jumped from my chair and slid the notecard back on the desk. Maybe time would jog my memory, but for now I had a story to get. Dotty Fitzgerald was a top contender for this year's bake off and if I could slither a few quotes out of her, it would be a great piece for my blog! I had to get to her before the bakery closed.

"Let me know if you ladies think of anything else," Declan said.

"We will," I said. "Thanks again, Declan, for everything."

I smiled as I backed away, and Gemma followed. I stepped into the hallway first, but Gemma lagged. I'd known her long enough that I should've been prepared for what came out of her mouth next.

"Yes, thank you detective handsome!" Gemma yelled and waved in his direction before she let his door close behind her. I shot her a glare. "What? Can't a girl have a little fun around here?"

There wasn't much I could do except laugh. I'd learned the first day I'd met her that Gemma had no filter. You always knew what she was thinking. That didn't stop my cheeks from turning as pink as the leaves on the dogwood trees outside the police station window.

CHAPTER EIGHTEEN

This whole case was getting stranger by the minute. My car crawled down the Main Street of Bluewater until I found an empty spot about a block up from Dotty's bakery. The writing on the notecard was still running through my mind.

"Who would Wanda trust enough to share her recipes with?" I asked.

"Well, like you said, her friend list is a lot shorter than her enemy list. Who in Blue Haven did Wanda get along with?" Gemma asked.

She was staring into the mirror on the visor. Her hand swiped a layer of lip gloss across her lips. I threw the car in park, cut the engine and looked over at her. Did Wanda have a Gemma? Everyone had to have a Gemma; there had to be someone Wanda confided in. I tried to write a list in my mind, but I couldn't get past number one. There was only one person I knew that genuinely liked Wanda.

"I guess it could've been Betty Jean," I said. "Maybe she wrote while Wanda baked."

"It's possible," Gemma said. She twisted the cap back on her lip gloss and unhooked her seatbelt. "You ready?"

I nodded and scanned the dark streets before opening the door. I didn't see any shadows, or a crazy person holding a baseball bat. It didn't make me any less uneasy as I opened the door. I gripped my keys tightly in my hand and walked quickly over to the sidewalk where Gemma was waiting. I wrapped my arm through hers and together we walked the one block back to Dotty's bakery.

The display case was almost empty when we walked inside and there was a woman checking out at the counter. A little boy stood next to her with his arms wrapped around her legs. She searched her purse for her wallet while holding onto a little girl. I glanced in the bakery case to see what was left while I waited.

"I call dibs on that last chocolate eclair," Gemma said.

"Good! I didn't want to have to fight you for that Mille-Feuille pastry," I laughed.

My eyes were locked on the zebra-like stripes that spanned the top of the pastry. My mouth was already watering thinking of the flakiness between each layer of cream. Next to the Mille-Feuille was one lonely mini quiche. I knew I'd have to snag that, too. Dotty was a strong contender for the Quiche on the Beach, and Von Reklaw had been getting a lot of emails asking what my opinion was.

"Hey, Dotty!" I waved. The other customer had snuck out of the bakery while I was salivating at the sweets.

"Hey there sugar. What brings you to Bluewater tonight?" Dotty asked.

I had to think quick. "She does," I said. I pointed at Gemma. "This is my friend Gemma. It's her first time visiting and I had to bring her over here, of course. She couldn't head back to New York without trying the best French bakery on this side of North Carolina."

"Well, aren't you sweet. What can I get for you two lovely ladies?"

Gemma and I both began pointing at our selections. Dotty swiped each dessert out of the case and set them into a white cardboard box for us to take with us. Being that it was only the three of us in the store, I decided now was a good time to dig a little deeper into the bake off and maybe even slip a few questions about Dotty's enhanced presence in Blue Haven.

"Did you hear that Mayor Allen announced the Quiche on the Beach Bake Off will go forward this year?" I asked.

"I sure did." Dotty tucked the sides of the box down inside and closed the top. "It feels criminal to be excited with all that's been going on."

"I can understand that, but this is your first year. That's a big deal. Do you have your recipe to perfection already?" I asked.

A smile appeared on Dotty's face. She slid the box onto the counter and began tapping away on the register. If Dotty's quiche was anything like her pastries, I could see why Suzy Atwater was agitated.

"I'd like to think so. My quiche goes where no quiche has gone before. You'll have to wait until the bake off to see how."

"I can't wait!" I could hear my voice rise. "Does it have anything to do with your visits to Blue Haven? I've seen you more this past week than the whole time I've lived here."

Dotty's smile faded. She closed the drawer to the cash register and began tidying up the papers that sat on the counter. The song playing through the speakers of the bakery ended and there was an eerie silence that filled the room. Gemma looked over at me. I shrugged and continued to watch Dotty shuffle the papers.

"It's kind of the reason," Dotty said. She looked up at me with narrow eyes. Her elbows lowered to the counter and she leaned in closer to Gemma and I. "I have a friend at the bank. She told me that Wanda's storefront would be going up for rent in the next few weeks. I've been wanting to open a store on the boardwalk of Blue Haven for years. It's rare that one goes up for rent and when it does I find out too late. She wanted to give me a heads-up. I went over there a few times to check it out. I peeked through the window and envisioned my idea."

"What's your idea?" I asked.

"Oh, I can't tell you that." Dotty pressed her finger to her lips.

I wanted to ask more questions, but the bell to the front door rang behind me before I could get another word out. I looked back to see a man and a woman holding hands. They walked up to the bakery case. I took that as my cue. Gemma pulled the box of pastries from the counter.

"We should probably get going," I said. "It was great to see you, Dotty."

"You too, my dear. Have a wonderful evening."

I held the door open for Gemma, who had the box gripped tightly against her chest. The sun had sunk closer to the horizon and hues of pink and purple now hovered over the quiet streets of Bluewater.

"Now what?" Gemma asked.

I looked over at her and tapped the top of the cardboard box. "Right now, we're going to go home and indulge in this box of pastries. Then, probably pass out on the couch."

Gemma and I laughed. I was ready to get home and spend some time not thinking about this investigation, even though I knew it would be short-lived. In the morning we were going to pay Ms. Betty Jean a visit. I had so many questions about that recipe card and Betty Jean might be the only one who had the answers.

CHAPTER NINETEEN

Forget Your Beach Bod When You Vacation Here in Blue Haven!

I know you've worked hard for those abs on your beach vacation, but I'm about to burst your bubble. You'll most likely leave with a little extra around that waistband after your trip to these shores. Don't feel guilty, though: the endless array of mouthwatering baked goods will be well worth it.

The fried cookie dough cart underneath the south pier is well worth the line you'll most likely have to wait in to get your hands on the goodies. Be sure to order more than one, because if you don't, I can guarantee you'll regret it as soon as you pop the first one in your mouth.

One of the best inventions here in Blue Haven is Java Jane's Brew Pops. The newest store at the end of the boardwalk serves cold brew on a stick. You can even add on specialty toppings. The amount of flavor combinations can be overwhelming, so if you trust me, top yours with caramel and sea salt. Mind blown, I know.

If you have time, hop in the car and head on over to Bluewater for the absolute best rendition of French pastries in the area. Stock up on goodies at Fitz's Patisserie. They'll make for a great snack on your car ride home when you're wallowing in the realization that your amazing beach vacation has come to an end. Be sure to tag Kaffeinated Kitchen in your socials if you visit and let me know what you ordered!

Love ya lattes,
Von Reklaw

***

The morning after I'd stuffed myself full of French pastries, I walked out of my house and down the steps past the wilting azaleas my grandmother had so proudly planted in memory of my grandfather. There were two reasons I'd decided to take Betty Jean up on her gardening tips offer. One of them was because I knew how much my grandmother had loved her azaleas; the second was, if anybody could give me inside information on Wanda, it was her.

It was almost 11 that morning, but Gemma was still sound asleep. Scout was staring at me from the window as I closed the fence behind me. The sky was overcast and the breeze sent a chill across the back of my neck as it blew past.

When I rounded the corner to her house, Betty Jean was sitting on her porch swing. She had a blanket over her lap and a mug in her hand. I waved to her, looked both ways, and then crossed the street. I could hear the eagerness in her voice when I'd called this morning to see if I could borrow her green thumb. She'd told me she would put on the coffee and that I could come whenever.

"Hi, Betty Jean," I yelled.

"Veronica, I'm so excited to see you," she said. "Your grandmother would be so happy you're following in her footsteps."

"I'm trying. I hope I can live up to her expectations," I said.

"Would you like some coffee before we get started?" Betty Jean asked.

"I would love some."

I did a double take when I followed Betty Jean inside her house. The interior was very similar to Wanda's. I eyed the beige wallpaper and velvet couch in the living room and wondered if they'd had the same interior decorator. Even the kitchen where the steaming coffee sat seemed eerily familiar, with the gray cabinets and white tile countertop. I leaned against the white tile while Better Jean searched for a mug from the cupboard above the coffee maker.

"How are you settling in, dear? I don't think I've asked you that lately." Betty Jean tipped the coffee pot and let a stream of dark roast pour into my cup.

"I'm doing well: my dog walking business is really taking off, the farmhouse is starting to feel like home, and Blue Haven is growing on me. Though I'm still a bit shaken over Wanda."

"I think we all are dear. It's really so sad." Betty Jean slid the now-filled mug toward me. "I know Wanda was difficult, but she had her moments. She was a good friend to me."

As long as I'd known Betty Jean, she'd been kind. It was rare for her to not have a smile on her face. Her lips were always painted with red lipstick, with a hint of pink on her cheeks. Betty Jean was the total opposite of Wanda, but if she could call Wanda a friend, I guess it's possible anyone in Blue Haven could've been one too.

"I imagine it's hard to know she's no longer next door," I said. She nodded. "Is there anyone you can talk to about it? Did you and Wanda ever spend time with anyone else in town?"

The stone look on her face changed. The corners of her lips curled up and a laugh escaped from between her lips. I wrapped my hands around the mug that was set in front of me as Betty Jean's laugh grew louder. It was contagious. I found myself laughing with her. The only thing was, I had no idea what I was laughing at.

"Don't get me wrong, I loved Wanda, but I know I'm one of the very few." Betty Jean said. "Others tolerated her when we went places together for my sake. Wanda was married to the cafe after she and Jerry divorced. She didn't care about whether or not people liked her and she was okay with the fact that most didn't."

"You can't think of anyone?" I asked.

Betty Jean shook her head. "Why do you ask, dear?"

I knew I couldn't go into detail about what I knew. Especially now that I knew someone was after me. I must have been getting close, and the way the town talked, I couldn't take any chances. I didn't want Betty Jean talking about the recipe card at one of her next bridge nights.

"No reason," I said. "It seems like with her love of cooking she'd have someone to work on new recipes with. Join a cooking club or something."

"Oh no! Not when it came to cooking. I learned that the hard way."

"What do you mean?" I asked.

"About a week before she was murdered, she was coming home much later than usual. Her headlights would flash through my bedroom window. The light startled me and I looked out and saw her. It was after midnight for three nights in a row. I confronted her about the annoyance and she apologized. She said she was at the cafe working on her quiche recipe. I'm nosey. I thought maybe she was dating. One night I went out. I drove to the cafe around eleven and the lights were on. The door was wide open. I heard voices from inside. They were coming from the back door, so they were muffled. I listened until the back door slammed and I tiptoed inside. Wanda was in the storage room. There was a lot of banging. I called out her name and she flew out of that room. She slammed the door behind her and didn't let go of the handle."

I took a sip of my coffee as I listened. Betty Jean said that Wanda had been livid that she'd shown up unannounced. She'd told Wanda they were even for all the nights Betty Jean had been woken up thanks to Wanda's headlights. Eventually Wanda had settled down. She'd locked the storage door before the two of them had left that night.

"Have you told the detective about the argument?" I asked.

"No, I suppose I haven't. I hadn't even thought about it until now." Betty Jean's hand shot up to her mouth. "Oh, what if—oh my!"

She stepped back and caught herself on the granite of the island counter. The color in her face faded and I could see the worry in her eyes.

"I should've pressed harder. Maybe she would've told me." Betty Jean let out a heavy sigh.

"You can't blame yourself," I said. The heat from my hand evaporated onto the skin of her shoulder where it was resting. "Wanda was stubborn. I don't think you would have been able to get the information out of her. You should make sure to tell Special Agent Grant, though."

Betty Jean nodded. I walked over to the sink, pulled open the cupboard above it and pulled out a glass so I could pour her some water. She drank it down and for the next hour we had a long gardening session. It was nice to take our minds off of Wanda for a little, but once we were done, Betty Jean hopped in her car to head to the police station. Me? I pulled out my phone, called Gemma and told her to meet me at the boardwalk. We had some breaking and entering to do.

CHAPTER TWENTY

It had been a few hours since I'd left Betty Jean's. I was waiting for Gemma, leaning against the wooden railing of the boardwalk, my eyes fixed on the roughness of the waves as they slammed into the shore. Their roar was so loud that I didn't even hear Gemma's heavy breathing once she arrived. Her hand fell heavy on my shoulder and I jolted my head in her direction. She wasn't alone. I swallowed hard, wondering how much trouble I was in that I hadn't yet made the call to Declan about Betty Jean's story.

"Veronica," the deepness of Declan's voice made me uneasy. I smiled waiting for an interrogation.

"I called Declan, like you told me to," Gemma interrupted. I looked over at her. Her eyes widened and with a half-smile, she winked at me.

"Yes," I nodded. "I—knew... you would want to be here once you heard what Betty Jean had to say."

"You bet," Declan said. "Though we went through that storage closet with a fine-tooth comb. I can't imagine we'll find anything new."

"I guess we're going to find out!" Gemma was already at the door to the old Savory Egg Cafe.

The yellow caution tape was hanging to one side, but the lock around the handle was still secure. The keys dangled in Declan's hands as he popped it open. He flipped on the lights and waited for the door to close behind us. The heaviness in my chest grew with each step I took into the half-empty cafe. I could see the dust that had settled on top of the wooden chairs that had still been left inside. It took a little more energy to take in air by the time I got behind the counter. It felt strange to stand where I'd stood the day I found Wanda. The only thing there today were crumbs on the gray concrete.

"You okay?" Declan asked.

I nodded, hoping the look on my face was convincing enough for him not to ask any more questions. It seemed to work. Even though the worry in his eyes didn't fade, he seemed to believe me enough to move on. I followed him to the door of the storage closet. I watched his hand firmly grasp the handle and slowly turn it until I heard the click. Declan flicked the light switch a few times, but it was no use. I didn't realize I had stopped breathing until Gemma jumped out from behind me, scaring me half to death.

"Gemma!" I yelled. She threw her hands up.

"Sorry, V!" She patted me on the back and sprinted through the open door. "What do you think we're looking for?"

"I have no idea," Declan said. He waved his flashlight in front of him. "Like I said, we searched this room top to bottom."

I felt my way around in the dark, trying to stay in line with Declan's flashlight. There wasn't much in the closet that seemed mysterious. There was a metal shelf which held the usual cafe ingredients such as flour, oil, condiments, and dishes. In the opposite corner were an empty mop bucket and a broom.

"This seems hopeless. There's nothing in here," I said. My hands were rummaging through the middle shelf. I pushed past a few hot sauce and maple syrup bottles. None seemed to be hiding any deep dark secrets.

"I'm not having any luck either." I looked over right as Gemma stepped her foot into a bucket. She screamed and Declan and I turned toward her. Neither of us was able to grab her before the brick wall caught her fall.

"Gemma, are you okay?!" I bent down beside her.

"I think so."

Gemma kicked the bucket off her foot and climbed her hands up the wall. Her right hand pushed against the brick and as she stood, I saw her hand slip. She looked back at the brick and pressed against it again. Gemma looked back at me wide-eyed.

"What is it?" I asked.

"This brick... it's loose." I looked over at Declan, who was now shining the light by Gemma's hand. Gemma felt around the rim of the brick. "Help me!"

I kept my eyes on Gemma as I made my way to her. She pried her fingers around one side of the brick, but her grip could not get it to come out. I looked around for something to help. There was a butter knife sitting on the metal shelf. I grabbed it and jammed it into the side of the brick, deep enough to be able to pull it out. Before I could wave Declan over, I felt the warmth of his breath on my shoulder. He poked the flashlight into the hole in the wall.

Gemma motioned for me to look inside, but all I could picture was the scary movies we'd watched in our apartment in the city. I was waiting for the creepy crawlies to bust out and take over my hand. I shook my head and my whole body shuddered.

"Alright, alright, I'll do it," Gemma said.

She shoved her hand inside and felt around. I held my breath as she pulled out her hand. Gripped between her fingers was a stack of papers. She handed them over to Declan and I watched over his shoulder as he flipped through them.

"They're all Wanda's recipes," he said.

I leaned in closer. There were dozens of quiche recipes. They were all in the same fancy handwriting we'd seen on the card at the station. Handwriting that I knew wasn't Wanda's. Declan handed over each piece of paper to me as he inspected it.

"Wait! What's that?" I said.

All the recipes were now in my hand. What Declan was holding was something different. I took the flashlight from his hand so he could juggle them all.

"Well?" Gemma asked.

"They're contracts." Declan flipped through a few more. "Between Wanda, and..."

Declan looked up at Gemma and me. His jaw hung open and I could tell by the way his forehead wrinkled that he wasn't expecting what he saw on the paper. He reached out his hand and Gemma snatched it before I could find the strength to move. She studied the signatures on each page and after a minute of analyzing it she thrust herself back against the wall and let out a huge gasp. Declan and I both looked over at a terrified Gemma.

"I knew I'd seen that handwriting before," she said. "It took me a minute because the card was in black and white. When I first saw the handwriting, it was in color. The words were in blue and pink and they were much bigger."

I still didn't know what Gemma was talking about, but my muscles finally decided to cooperate. I took the papers from Gemma's hand and studied the name signed next to Wanda's.

"Oh my gosh!" I yelled. I shot my hand up to my mouth. Gemma wasn't the only one who'd seen that writing before. I'd seen it too. The other day on the boardwalk when in big bold letters, that same person, in that same handwriting had written: *Buy One, Get One.*

CHAPTER TWENTY-ONE

The Secret to the Perfect Quiche Crust!

Kaffeinated Kitchen is beyond excited to share this week's blog post! It comes from none other than the Queen of Quiche herself, Wanda Hemmings! Unless you've been hiding under a rock for the last nine years, you know that Wanda is unbeatable when it comes to mastering the perfect quiche. That's why we are thrilled that Wanda is giving us tips on how to make the perfect crust from scratch. Her apple and brie quiche left the judges salivating at last year's bake off and although she won't fully reveal the secrets of that recipe, she is spilling the beans (or should I say eggs) to help you master your crust.

Get your pens ready—here's the recipe:

Crust Ingredients:

4 cups flour
2 tsp salt
1 ¾ cup shortening
½ cup ice water
1 tsp cider vinegar
1 large egg

Directions:

Grab a small mixing bowl. Start whisking together the egg, vinegar and ice water. After that, pull out your food processor. First, you'll add flour and salt. Give it a few quick pulses and then add in the shortening. Pulse again until mixed and pour in the egg mixture. Start the processor again until the dough starts to form. When your dough is ready, sprinkle some flour onto an open space on your counter and scoop the dough onto it. Roll out the dough to fit the size of your baking dish. Then, ever so gently lift the dough from the counter and place on top of your dish. Press the dough into place and cut off any overhang. Place the dough in the refrigerator to chill. Wanda says her magic number is 2 hours, but chill for at least 30 minutes. Pull from the fridge and TA DA! Your quiche crust is ready to be filled and baked.

I can already smell new entries for the next Quiche on the Beach Bake Off with this recipe!

Love ya lattes,
Von Reklaw

***

The contracts in my hand dated back almost a decade. The same two names were on the bottom of all of them. I skimmed them to try and figure out what in the heck was going on and when I was done, I was more confused than ever.

"Wanda was buying her quiche recipes!" I was shocked. "Mae Wicks is the real quiche queen."

The reigning champion of the Quiche on the Beach Bake Off had been a fraud. Every single one of the contracts in my hand bought two things: quiche and silence. Darn her for making Von Reklaw look like a fool.

"Do you think Mae hurt Wanda?" Gemma asked.

"If these contracts are real. Wanda and Mae have been running this scheme for pretty much the entirety of the bake off. Why would Mae want to hurt Wanda now? After all this time?" I wondered.

"Maybe she got tired of being silent," Declan said. "You said that Mae was the first to arrive that morning, correct?" I nodded. "How long do you think it took her to show up?"

I tried to think back to that morning. I remembered seeing the envelope on the counter. I called out for Wanda and then I saw the stove. The clock! I had looked up at it before I noticed the stove. It was only moments after that that I'd found Wanda's body. The shock was followed by my scream, my fall into the wall, and my purse crashing to the ground.

"No more than two minutes," I said. Declan pulled out his notebook. His gaze alternated between the writing inside and the direction of Mae's store. "What is it?" I asked.

"When I originally interviewed her, she said she was in her nightgown doing her hair, but that morning she was dressed in jeans and a t-shirt," Declan said. "I find it hard to believe it took all of two minutes to change, run down the stairs, across the street, and over to the cafe in that amount of time."

Declan was making a good point. For a professional athlete, that might be possible, but Mae carried a lot of weight on her, and she was in her late fifties. At that moment, I also remembered when Mae's curlers had poked against the side of my head. They weren't hot or even warm. They were cool to the touch as if she'd had them in for some time by then.

"That would make sense!" I gasped.

"What would?" Gemma asked.

"If it really is Mae, it would make since that she was the one in the alley that night. She lives right across the street. She definitely could have heard the two of us coming. The noise would've traveled right up to her window. The reason I heard no car when the shadow disappeared would be because she didn't need one," I said.

"I'm going to go ask Mae a few questions and see what I can get out of her. You two stay here," Declan ordered.

"You can't be serious," Gemma balked.

"I am. If Mae was the one that attacked you, we don't know what she'll do if she feels cornered. I don't want to take the chance of the two of you getting hurt."

"Look at you, detective... handsome and a gentleman," Gemma joked. I rolled my eyes. Leave it to her to find something amusing in a serious situation.

"We'll wait here," I said.

I meant what I said, but I should've known the crime lover in Gemma wouldn't hold back. We watched Declan walk across the street and she gave Declan a five-second head start before she started yanking me closer to the front door. The sun was setting by then. There were still a few vacationers enjoying meals outside on the patios of some of the restaurants, but most of the shops were closed by now. Mae's would be closing soon, too.

"There's no one inside," she said.

"Do you see Mae?" I asked.

Gemma nodded. I was a few feet behind her with my back pressed up against the brick wall. My chest was heavy from the current pounding where my heart normally beat.

"What's going on?" I was too afraid to move, but curiosity was getting the best of me.

"I can't hear anything. I have to go in there," she said.

"Gemma, no!"

I lunged at her when she started to move, but the six inches that she had on me and the extra workout classes she'd been taking meant I was no match. She flung her arm out of my grasp, grabbed my hand, and yanked me inside.

We hid behind a tall display of evergreen candles stacked into the shape of a tree.

"Can you see him?" Gemma whispered.

I jerked my finger up to my lips. The sound of mellow instrumentals floated through the loudspeakers. I didn't hear any voices, but I could see around the candles. Declan was slowly making his way up to the register. I looked over at Gemma and pointed to the next display of stacked candles that was closer to the front of the room. She winked, slipped out from behind the evergreen candles and we both tiptoed to the closer display so we could hear.

"Good afternoon, Ms. Wicks," Declan said.

Gemma and I both looked at each other. A smile graced my face. I'd only learned of Mae's last name when I had read the contracts, but it didn't dawn on me until now how fitting it was for her store. That is something that only happens here in Blue Haven.

"Can I help you?" Mae asked.

"My name is Special Agent Grant. I'm not sure if you remember me. I'm working on the Wanda Hemmings case and was wondering if I could ask you a few questions."

Mae nodded but didn't make direct eye contact with Declan. She was busy straightening up the boxes that sat on the counter. I still couldn't believe that we were standing inside Scented Wicks possibly staring at Wanda's killer.

"Do you recognize this?" Declan asked.

I watched him place something onto the counter. It looked to be plastic and I could only assume it was the recipe card. Mae stopped straightening the box and turned to look down at it. She bent down to get a closer look.

"Doesn't look familiar," she said.

"How about this?" Declan set the bottle of perfume next to the recipe card. Mae shook her head.

"Ms. Wicks, who wrote the words on the sign outside your door?" Declan asked.

"Why do you ask?" Mae's voice began to rise. Declan pointed at another sign that sat on the counter. It was written in the same handwriting.

"Ms. Wicks, this is the same handwriting that was used on this recipe card. This recipe card was found with Wanda Hemmings the morning she was killed."

"Are you accusing me of killing Wanda?" Mae slapped her hands over her chest and gasped.

"Should I be?" Declan asked.

"Get out of my store!" Mae yelled. "How dare you come in here accusing me of such nonsense."

I don't know what came over me, but in that moment, I used the chaos to make a run for Mae's apartment. I left Gemma standing behind the candle display and I ran to the stairs. I turned behind me as I tiptoed up the wooden stairs to see Mae's back was still to me. She was too focused on getting Declan out of the store.

I took a deep breath at the top and slowly turned the handle into Mae's apartment. I opened the door just enough to slither my way inside. I looked around, but had no idea what I was looking for. I started at the desk next to the door. Nothing. Then I moved to the nightstand. Still nothing. My heart was pounding so loud I was afraid the sound would overpower any footsteps coming up the stairs. I gently closed the drawer to the nightstand and turned around. A large cherry oak armoire sat on the opposite side of Mae's studio.

I walked quickly over and started sorting through the drawers. I stopped when I came to the top. My eyes shot open. Inside was not one, but two bottles of Lavender Delight. I went to reach for it, but came to my senses before my hands touched them. Instead, I took out my phone, snapped a quick pic and with a tissue, I grabbed two of the makeup brushes that sat on top of the armoire.

My time in Mae's apartment had come to an end, but I had no idea how I was going to get out. I pulled my phone out again and sent an SOS to Gemma. I wasn't sure if she was still downstairs or not. She replied with a simple thumbs up and within a minute I heard a loud commotion outside followed by a familiar scream. I ran to the window to see Gemma on the ground next to the A-frame sign in front of Mae's store. Mae was squatting down next to her. Without hesitation, I ran out of the apartment, down the stairs and out the back door that led into the alley. I barely had time to catch my breath when I felt something hard hit my arm.

"Are you crazy?" I turned around to find Declan glaring at me.

"It's her. Mae is the one who tried to attack us in the alley. I found more bottles of Lavender Delight in her room."

"You're lucky she didn't kill you for real up in her apartment. What were you thinking?"

Declan's tone was terse. His grip was unwavering on my arm.

"I'm sorry," I said. "But I did swipe these for you. Maybe they have fingerprints?"

"Maybe—but I can't submit stolen goods as evidence."

"Right... I didn't think about that."

"I respect the effort," Declan said. "Next time, let me do my job. Okay?"

"Deal," I said. "I should probably go save Gemma now."

I handed Declan the makeup brushes and waved to him as I walked down the alley to where I could still hear commotion from the sidewalk. When I peeked around the corner, Gemma was in full drama mode. Mae, Mr. Gordon and a few others surrounded her.

"I think it's broken," she yelled. Then she noticed me walking toward her. She rubbed her hands over her ankle a few more times. "Actually, it's starting to feel much better."

"It was probably shock," Mr. Gordon said. "You should get that checked out."

I stepped in. "Oh my gosh! Gemma, what happened?"

"Texting and walking." Gemma shrugged. "I ran right into this sign."

"We should get you checked out," I said. I bent down and let Gemma wrap her arm around me. She winced and hobbled up on one foot.

"No, no, really, I'm fine. See."

Miraculously, Gemma's broken ankle was healed. She bore her weight on it and two-stepped around me. She thanked everyone for their help and pushed me quickly away from the crowd. Once we were no longer in earshot, she let me have it. She slapped my forearm and the sting lingered.

"What were you thinking?!" Gemma yelled.

"I wasn't. I only knew I had to get up there," I said.

"And...?"

"And I'm certain Mae was the one who tried to attack us. I found Lavender Delight in her apartment. I'm sorry, but this is Blue Haven. No one in this town is up on the latest perfume trends. She has to be the one."

"Anything to prove she killed Wanda?" Gemma asked.

I shook my head. There wasn't really any hard evidence to put Mae at the scene of the crime. The only thing I could hope was that there were fingerprints on that makeup brush. That would confirm it, but even then, like Declan had said, he couldn't use stolen goods to arrest someone. We were still out of luck when it came to bringing Wanda's killer to justice.

CHAPTER TWENTY-TWO

"I don't think obsessively checking your phone will get those fingerprints processed any faster, but it will surely melt your ice cream," Gemma said, pointing in my direction.

I could feel the stickiness of my chocolate scoop running down my hand. I grabbed the napkin on my lap and stopped it in time from dripping onto my white shorts. Declan had told me he'd call as soon as he had any answers, but almost an entire day had gone by since I'd escaped from Mae's apartment with her makeup brush, and my phone hadn't rung since.

"I can't help it. I need to know if Mae's fingerprints match," I said. "Don't you want to know if she's the one who tried to whack you with a baseball bat?"

"Of course, I do!" Gemma whispered. "But while you sit over there dwelling on it, I'm going to enjoy my ice cream and wait for Declan to do what he said he was going to do. He will call."

"I know." I sighed and leaned back onto the bench. "Ouch!"

I'd forgotten it was the middle of the day and the sun had been beating down since 9am. I'd jumped from the bench, stumbled to find my footing, and lost one of my flip-flops in the process. Now the bottom of my right foot was roasting on concrete submerged in the peak of the summer sun.

"Veronica!" I could hear Gemma laughing as I hopped around trying to figure out where I'd kicked my other flip-flop. "Stand still. I've got you!"

Gemma slid my lost flip-flop on my foot and after I'd caught my balance, I saw the aftermath. My hand was now gripping an empty waffle cone. The scoop of chocolate ice cream was running down the crack of the concrete. That was probably my karma for sticking my nose where it didn't belong.

"Well, I guess that's my cue. I've got to get over to Peaches for the Quiche on the Beach press conference anyway. I'm pretty sure the whole town will be crowded inside and I need to get close enough for my phone to record," I said.

"Ah, that's how you do it," Gemma said. "I wondered how you stayed incognito."

"Yeah, it's much easier that way. Plus, I was always a horrible notetaker. Do you know how many times I mixed up information when I was working the blotter back in New York? One time I wrote about the bodega being robbed with a bouquet of flowers," I said.

Gemma laughed. I tossed my empty waffle cone in the trash and the two of us headed down the boardwalk to Peaches.

***

It seemed that even though Wanda's killer was still running free, most of Blue Haven had returned to normal. The crowd inside Peaches was full of chatter. As Gemma and I pushed our way through, I could hear echoes of conversations surrounding me.

"Suzy Atwater is a shoe-in!" I heard a young blonde in an oversized straw hat say. She was rebutted by an older man with glasses.

"My money is on Dotty. I can't get enough of her crepes. I can only imagine what her quiche is going to taste like."

Both Dotty and Suzy were lingering by the microphone near the front counter of the cafe. I held my breath to fit through the open spaces of the crowd.

"Oh! Oh! I see two spots over there!" Gemma yelled.

She grabbed my hand and yanked me forward. I winced at the feeling of her nails gripping in my skin as the two open seats grew closer. When we'd finally claimed them, I could see the imprint of Gemma's nails in my palm. Before I could make any jokes about her hulk-like strength Mayor Allen was calling for everyone's attention.

"We are now a couple of weeks away from the commencement of the tenth annual Quiche on the Beach Bake Off!" The crowd erupted in applause. I took that opportunity to press record on my phone before I slipped it back into my purse. "This event here in Blue Haven has become a staple. People from all over the southeast come to enjoy good weather, good food and good company. Today, I would like to officially introduce you to our bake off contestants."

One by one Mayor Allen introduced all the contestants. There were seven in total. I looked down to make sure the timer on my phone was still going as each one took to the microphone to give a shoutout and take a few questions. This was always the part where I had to get creative. Being that I, Veronica Walker, wasn't a journalist in this town, I had to finagle someone else to ask questions for me. When Dotty stepped up to the mic, I swept my hair off my shoulders and loudly whispered over to Gemma, "I wonder how Dotty feels going up against such a veteran as Suzy Atwater." Gemma winked and I noticed a reporter from the county paper's hand shoot up.

"Dotty, tell us, how are you keeping it together, knowing that you're going up against someone like Ms. Atwater?"

Dotty leaned into the microphone. "It's an honor to be able to compete at the same level as someone as talented as Suzy. I'd like to think I have a few tricks up my sleeve to be able to hold my own next week. I guess we'll just have to taste and see." A giggle escaped from Dotty's lips as she stepped back and traded places with Evelyn Hammonds.

I was getting ready to lean in again toward Gemma when a bell rang out from inside my purse. I swept my purse from the floor, flung it onto my lap and grabbed my phone.

"Is it Declan?" Gemma whispered. I looked down to see the name flashing across my phone.

"It is." I held my breath and swiped my finger to read the message.

Declan: Results are in. Meet me at the station.

I turned to Gemma. "We have to go!"

I didn't explain, but by the way she jumped from her seat I knew I didn't have to. We squeezed our way back out of the crowd to the front door and hurried to the station. The results were in. We were about to find out if it was Mae after all who'd tried to leave us for dead right on the very boardwalk we were now running down.

CHAPTER TWENTY-THREE

The same brown-haired woman was sitting behind the desk of the police station when Gemma and I flung the door open. We were gasping for air with each step. The woman shook her head and waved us through. I was wildly aware of the mess I was as I walked down that hallway. My hair clung to my bottom lip and there was a rock poking the bottom of my heel. I tried to push the sharp pain out of my head. Declan was standing in the doorway to greet us.

"Thanks for coming so quickly," he said. "Come on in."

I'd caught my breath by the time I fell into the leather chair. Gemma sat next to me and Declan followed suit on the other side of the desk. His fingers skimmed over lines of paper in front of him and I impatiently pulled my chair closer.

"The suspense is killing me!" I said. "What did you find out?"

"We were able to pull fingerprints from the makeup brush and they are a match to both the frying pan and the perfume bottle. It's not looking good for Mae," Declan said.

"But you said it yourself, that's not really enough to bring her in, right?" Gemma asked.

"Technically, that's correct,' Declan said. "The paperwork we found, though, along with the fingerprints may be enough for probable cause. That's why you two are here."

This was it! The chance Gemma and I had been waiting for. Declan was finally going to let us have our CSI moment. I didn't know what he was going to let us do, but I pictured Gemma reading Mae her rights and me slapping the cuffs on her wrists. Okay, maybe that was overkill, but it sounded cool. I slapped my hands together waiting for my assignment. I was half excited and half petrified at the same time.

"I had an officer head over to her shop about an hour ago to bring her in for questioning. Her shop was closed. She wasn't in her apartment and we haven't been able to locate her. Until we find her, I need you two to be on high alert."

Whatever excitement I had drummed up two minutes ago had dissipated. I was now fully petrified. I felt like my own lungs were handcuffed. I tried to breathe, but couldn't take in any air. Declan's words echoed in my ears. *We haven't been able to locate her. I need you two to be on high alert.* Suddenly, I wanted to barricade myself in my house and curl up in bed with Scout and a dozen baseball bats.

I looked over at Gemma. Her normally tan complexion was gone. She was now the same color as the cream suede of the purse she was holding. I couldn't help but feel horrible as the terror on Gemma's face grew. This was all my fault. She was in this mess thanks to me.

"I'm going to have an officer on watch in your neighborhood just in case. I recommend holding off on the dog walking for the time being." The fear pouring out of my eyes must've been apparent to Declan now. "I'm not going to let anything happen to you two, okay?"

Gemma and I both nodded.

I pressed my hands against the arms of the chair and lifted what felt like ten of me to my feet. I walked as slowly as I could down the hallway. I knew once we were outside those walls anything could happen. *Where the heck had Mae gone?* If she knew the evidence was starting to point in her direction, it seemed smarter for her to run, not come after me. That logic lightened the heaviness in my chest as I pushed open the door of the station into the thick heat of the afternoon.

"It looks like we'll be shackled up in your house for the foreseeable future," Gemma said.

"I guess so," I muttered.

I wonder if the officer slowly rolling behind us in his four door sedan would let me take a detour to the grocery store. I wasn't one to stock my pantry in case of an emergency. My pantry shelves were pretty much empty and my fridge had some wilting lettuce, expired bottles of salad dressing and enough milk to maybe get a bowl of cereal out of. If Mae didn't kill me, starvation while waiting for her to try definitely would. I guessed I could wait to make sure we survived the first night and then worry about food in the morning.

"Are you hungry?" Gemma asked. It must've been best-friend ESP having her think of food at the same time.

"Kind of," I said.

"It looks like there's a burger place a few miles from here that delivers. I can put in an order if you want."

Delivery. *Duh.* I let out a huge sigh that I no longer had to add starvation to my list of worries. I may not have wanted to venture out to the boardwalk for a few days, but thanks to modern technology the boardwalk could still come to me.

"Let's do it!" I said. "I'll take a cheeseburger with extra cheese and a side of fries."

Gemma tapped her fingers on the glass of her phone a few times. She sent the order right as we were coming up to the end of my street. A few more yards to the bottom of the hill and we'd be safe and sound in my house.

"Hey there, Veronica." I looked up to the sound of a raspy voice to find Mr. Gordon walking our way.

"Hi, Mr. Gordon, how are you?" I asked.

"Oh, you know, same old, same old. And by that, I do mean old."

Gemma laughed. "I like him." She reached her hand out to meet his. "Gemma Becker."

"Nice to officially meet you. I'm Murphy Gordon."

"Thanks for saving my life the other day," Gemma laughed.

I watched as in the distance the officer pulled along the sidewalk a few houses down from mine. I could see a few curtains open and faces peer in the opening. I was in as much shock as they were that any cop had to be on patrol in this town. I could imagine the phone calls my neighbors were making to each other.

"Do you think there's been another murder?"

"Maybe Officer Flynn fancies someone on this street?"

"Oh, a booty call, eh?"

Yup, that all seemed pretty accurate. I was surprised Mr. Gordon hadn't noticed the car, and to be honest I wanted to get inside before he did. Declan had been clear that no one else could know what was going on, and I hated keeping secrets from Mr. Gordon. He had always been too sweet to me.

"I think our food should be here soon, right Gemma?" I asked.

She looked down at her phone. "Yup. Two more minutes."

"We should get going, then. It was so nice to see you, Mr. Gordon," I said.

"You too, Veronica. Give Scout a little pat on the head for me."

I assured him that I would. Scout would appreciate it. I let Mr. Gordon make the first move and once he started walking Gemma and I scurried the rest of the way down the hill, through the white fence and into the farmhouse. I had double-bolted the front door before Scout even made his way downstairs to the foyer. He sniffed frantically at my heels as I petted his curly coat the way Mr. Gordon had asked me to.

"Well, I guess we are in for an epic girls' night," Gemma said. "Burgers, a handsome yet furry man, and—maybe a chick flick?"

"Definitely a chick flick," I laughed.

That was the perfect remedy for a night like this. I would've given anything for that quiet night on the couch watching a chick flick and eating my weight in French fries, but the continuous chill on the back of my neck and the churning in my stomach had me thinking this night was going to be anything but relaxing.

CHAPTER TWENTY-FOUR

By nine o'clock that evening Gemma and I had watched three chick flicks, eaten our burgers and even made a batch of chocolate chip cookies that were sitting in the middle of the coffee table. Scout hadn't taken his eyes off of them and was obviously waiting for an opportunity when I wasn't looking to snatch one. I didn't give him that satisfaction. He was now nudging his cold nose under my arms.

"Do you need to go outside?" I asked. He started prancing around like a horse and whining. His nose nudged me again." Okay, let's go."

The night had been relatively quiet. I'd peeked out the window during the longwinded scenes of each movie to see if Officer Flynn was still perched out on the sidewalk. He was. I slipped Scout's collar over his head and he ran to the back door off the kitchen. The moon was glistening into the yard and when I flipped on the porch light it almost looked as if morning were seeping in. Scout didn't wait for me to wave him on. As soon as I opened the door he burst through.

"Gemma, do you want anything while I'm up?" I shouted.

"Maybe a glass of wine?" she asked.

"Red or white?"

"Surprise me!" Gemma said.

I bent down to the wine fridge and opened the door. Sadly, I couldn't take credit for the fully stocked selection. My grandmother had always been the wine lover. She'd had a subscription to a few wineries in the Carolinas and had left those to me as well. Each month when they arrived, I stuck them in the fridge, but I'd never had any real reason to open a bottle. Gemma on the other hand—she'll fabricate any excuse. I flipped over a few bottles until one of the labels caught my eye. It was pale pink with foil gold lettering. If the label was pretty that had to mean the wine was good. That was my thought process anyway.

I pulled the bottle from the shelf and admired what turned out to be a Riesling from the western Carolina mountains.

The wine glasses were on the shelf above the stove. I pressed the bottom of my toes into the floor and went to reach for the glasses when I heard Scout start to bark. I pulled back and ran to the window. His barking was full force now and when I looked outside I saw the back gate open. Scout was standing a few feet from it. I never opened that gate.

"Gemma!" I yelled, walking to the back door. I started to clap my hands. I wanted to get Scout's attention and also to warn anyone who might be on the other side of that fence that I was there.

"What's wrong?" Gemma asked.

I turned towards her to explain when suddenly, Scout's barking stopped. I jerked my head toward the yard. He was gone. The gate was still open. For a second, my entire body was still. I tried to move, but it was as if I were encased in concrete. Then the thought of my dog out there alone came tumbling into my mind. I looked back at Gemma.

"Call Declan. Get Officer Flynn. Tell him to head down Oakwood Street."

"Wait what? Where are you going?" Gemma asked.

"To get my dog!"

I bolted out the door, leaped down the wooden stairs and sprinted across the long lawn and through the open gate. I didn't care about the crunch under my bare feet or of any baseball bats that may come flying at me. If Mae really was out there, she wasn't messing with Veronica Walker anymore. She was messing with Scout's Mom and when it came to my dog, I'd gladly fight to the death to save him.

I made as much noise as I could when I turned on Oakwood Street so that Scout could hear me. I wanted him to know I was coming. I was looking for him. The thought of him out there in the dark without me was more terrifying than getting attacked.

The streets were quiet with the exception of one solo car passing me. I yelled for Scout again, but heard nothing. I ran further down the street to where the woods met the fork in the road and listened. It was faint, but I'd know that whimper from anywhere. It was coming from the woods.

"Grams, if you're up there. I could really use your help right now," I said. Then, I took a deep breath and went for it. I charged into the woods. "Scout! Scout, come here buddy!" I yelled.

In one fell swoop he came galloping at me. I felt the tears in my eyes. I bent down and let him lift his dirt filled paws onto me. My arms hugged him tighter than ever before.

"My little baby, I'm so glad you're okay," I said.

"Of course, he's okay," a stern voice yelled through the dark. "It's not the dog I'm after."

I gripped my hand around Scout's collar and stood up. The large shadow grew closer until a figure appeared.

"Mae. I knew it," I said. "Why?"

"I never wanted to hurt you, Veronica."

With each step Mae took closer, I took one back. I clenched my fist and hoped enough time had passed that Declan and Officer Flynn would be close by. I talked as loud as I could in hopes that they'd hear me.

"You tried to steal my dog."

"No. I knew you'd come after him and I needed to get you alone. I need you to understand."

"Understand what?" I asked.

"It was an accident," Mae blubbered. "I didn't mean to."

"You didn't mean to what?" I asked.

Mae pulled her hands from behind her back and raised them toward me. That's when I saw a small flicker in her grip. Mae was pointing a gun right at me.

"All these years, those recipes, they were mine," Mae said. "Wanda paid me for my quiche recipes, but this year, I decided I was going to enter myself. Wanda was furious. This would be her tenth win and she didn't want me to take that away from her. I threatened to go public with the fact that she was a fake, but she said no one would believe the candle shop owner over the cafe owner."

I looked down at Scout. His eyes were locked on Mae. I couldn't believe what I was hearing. The tears falling from Mae's eyes seemed genuine, but the way her hands were shaking made the hair across my whole body stand up. I stepped back again to steady myself so I could listen further.

"And then what happened?" I asked. I wasn't sure if she was telling the truth, but I was willing to listen to her story.

"She stormed out of my shop but came back the next day to apologize. We shook on it. She was going to let me enter, but she meant none of it. She asked to use the restroom before she left. I didn't realize until the next morning that she'd snuck up to my apartment and stolen the recipe."

"And you're sure it was her?" I asked.

"I'm positive. I know it was. I was fuming. I looked out the window and I saw her front door open that morning. I marched over there and saw her about to use my recipe to whip up some quiche. I demanded that she give me my recipe back. When she refused, I ran behind the counter and tried to grab it from her. She was taunting me, waving the recipe in the air. After multiple unsuccessful attempts at yanking her arm, I reached behind me and grabbed the skillet. I wasn't going to hit her with it. I only wanted to scare her, but she jumped back. She tripped and tried to catch her balance, but she fell. Her head hit the counter on the way down. It was an accident."

Mae could no longer control herself. Her entire body was shaking. The tears were streaming down her face. I felt my jaw drop. Out of the corner of my eye, I noticed that Mae and I weren't alone. Declan was standing behind a large tree. Mae was too busy crying to notice. He put his finger to his lips. His other hand was gripping his phone and I knew then that I needed to keep Mae talking.

"If it was an accident, why go through all this trouble to cover it up?"

"I panicked. She was lying there. She wasn't moving. I didn't know what to do. I hurriedly wiped the handle of the skillet and I placed it on the floor beside her and I ran. When I heard you scream, I knew I had to go back. I had to see for myself that she really was... dead."

"And then you tried to attack me, Mae! For what? What did I do to you?"

The look in Mae's eyes hollowed. Her lip quivered as she stepped toward me. I heard the click as Mae's finger slid on the gun. I put my hands up and with my leg I pushed Scout behind me.

"I never wanted to hurt you," she said. "I only wanted to scare you. I saw you at the Farmers Market and I heard you and your friend talking the other day while you were in the store about knocking suspects off your list. You were getting too close. I've spent my whole life in other people's shadows. I wanted my moment. I wanted to win the bake off and if you figured out I was there, in Wanda's cafe, if I went down for her death, I'd never be able to prove myself."

The words coming out of Mae's mouth sent a wave of relief through me. The last twenty-four hours Gemma and I had jumped at the slightest noises. We'd turned around after every step we'd taken, wondering if someone were following us. I had felt unsafe in Blue Haven for the first time since I'd arrived. I hated to know that the silhouette in the alley was Mae and I still couldn't completely comprehend that she was standing in front of me pointing a gun at my face.

"You said so yourself, Mae, it was an accident. You didn't kill Wanda. She fell. The police will understand that."

I had no idea if that was true, but with Scout's whimpering getting louder and Mae getting closer, I had to do something. I needed Mae to put that gun down.

"They won't understand. No one understands. Wanda was a witch. She took and took and took. I let her have everything. The prize money, the title, and the reputation. I wanted one year and she couldn't give that to me."

"That's where you're wrong," I said. "The bake off is still on for this year. There's still time. Put the gun down, Mae, and we'll figure it out. We'll figure out how to fix it."

Mae's lower lip quivered, catching the rivers running down her face. Her hands were still shaking, but I could see her shoulders fall. I nodded as she bent to the ground and set the gun on the dirt. Silence blew through the woods for a minute until Mae stood back up and stepped far enough from the gun that I was no longer in danger. Officer Flynn and Declan charged from their hiding spots.

"Ms. Wicks," Declan stepped out from behind the tree with his gun raised. "I need you to put your hands up and turn around slowly. "

Mae nodded. She didn't put up a fight. She pulled her hands up and when Declan got close enough he slid the handcuffs from his back pocket and put them around each of her wrists. I watched as the two of them walked over the dead branches to the street. I couldn't help but feel bad for Mae. I knew Wanda was a hard person to get along with but to steal recipes and pass them off as her own all these years? Then to threaten the poor woman for wanting to enter her recipes into the bake off under her own name? I could only imagine the gossip that would be spilling around town once all this came out.

Scout and I walked back out into the street to find Gemma running frantically at us. She threw her arms around me.

"Oh my gosh, Veronica, I was so scared!"

"I'm okay," I said. "Thank you for getting me help."

Officer Flynn walked over with a bottle of water. He bent down and tipped the bottle for Scout to drink. I still had a death-grip on his collar. He was never leaving my sight again.

"Are you okay, Ms. Walker?" Officer Flynn asked. I nodded. "Want me to give you ladies a ride back to the house? I can take your statements there."

"Sure," I said. I walked over to the police car and let Scout in first. Gemma and I followed.

"Did that just happen?" Gemma asked.

"It sure did," I said.

"I could really use that glass of wine, now," Gemma said.

I laughed. That seemed like the perfect way to end this crazy day. Officer Flynn closed us in the backseat and took us back to my house, where after giving our statements, we indulged in the entire bottle of white wine and fell into the first blissful sleep we'd had in days.

CHAPTER TWENTY-FIVE

If You're Not in Blue Haven Right Now, You're Missing Out!

The big day has finally come! Set your alarms for bright and early so you get the best seat possible. Tomorrow some of the best bakers in the state of North Carolina will be competing to be Queen of the Quiche right here in our lovely Blue Haven!

Shock is still among us as we cope with the fact that Wanda Hemming's drool-worthy quiches weren't her concoction after all. This year, we start fresh and the competition is fierce. Suzy Atwater is confident that her newest recipe will wow the judges, and I know patrons of Peaches Cafe can't wait until it's added to the regular menu.

If you've never attended the Quiche on the Beach Bake Off before, we're so glad you're here. Bring your appetites and your stretch pants. After the competition is over, you'll get to try the competitors' creations for yourself. Get ready, get set, it's almost time for the bake off! See you in the morning, quiche lovers.

Love ya lattes,
Von Reklaw

***

The Quiche on the Beach Bake Off had finally arrived, and with everything that had happened since Mae had been arrested, I knew I was thankful for a fun distraction. Gemma had ended up staying longer than she'd planned. I'd put my dog walking duties on hold for a bit so I could wrap my head around the fact that I'd found a body and helped catch a murderer. Well, a sort-of murderer anyway.

With Gemma still in Blue Haven, I had a great excuse to test out new menu items around town for my blog. I'd even started a new section called *Pour Me* where I gave the lowdown on all things wine. My grandmother would have been proud. It was driving tons of new traffic to my blog and I'd even secured a few food brands that wanted to advertise on my site. My dreams were starting to come true, and even with a slight hiccup along the way I owed it all to the tiny town of Blue Haven.

Contrary to its name, the Quiche on the Beach Bake Off didn't take place directly on the beach. The Surf's Up Cafe opened its doors for the event every year. Their back patio overlooked the beach and offered direct access for quiche lovers to take their samples onto the sand to enjoy.

Inside the cafe it was pretty packed. The bake off was about to start. Suzy was preparing her station, as were the rest of the bakers. There was a large plastic sign that hung above. It read: *Celebrating 10 Years!* At the bottom of the same banner, there was another strip that dedicated this event to Blue Haven's finest. If you were to tear that strip up, you'd see the original dedication with Wanda's name on it.

It turns out Wanda had been wrong. The town did believe Mae's story about selling her quiche recipes to Wanda. Suzy Atwater had relished it the most, but after a few days, saying her name became taboo. Wanda's legacy was buried with her. They even took the sign down above the door of her cafe. It was rumored that Dotty Fitzgerald had officially signed on the dotted line of the now-vacant location to open a French toastery.

"Alright, contestants," Mayor Allen yelled, "you will have one hour to prepare and bake your quiche. I will ring the bell at the thirty and forty-five-minute mark. I'll give you a five-minute warning. Good luck. The countdown will begin now."

Mayor Allen turned to the crowd and held his hands up. We all shouted, three, two, one, bake off! That's when the knives came out and the chopping began. I snapped a few photos before Gemma and I snuck out for some air.

"Are you sure you can't stay a little longer?" I asked Gemma, once we were down on the beach.

"I'm afraid not, but I am glad to hear that I haven't worn out my welcome," she said. "How about you? Will you be staying here a little longer?"

I'd done a lot of thinking about the job offer in New York. It would be a great opportunity for me. There would be someone else paying for all the meals I'd be eating. My write-ups would be seen by thousands of people a day, not to mention the doors that would open for me back in New York City. I would be a fool to pass it up.

"I know it sounds crazy," I said, "but I like it here." I bent down to pick up a white seashell. "No one knew me better than my grandmother, and the more time I spend down here, the more I realize why she gave me that farmhouse."

"Really? Why?" Gemma asked.

"She always told me that I had the entrepreneurial spirit. That I was going to do big things one day. Be my own boss. Down here I feel like that could happen. I mean, my blog made enough this month to pay my bills and maybe even let me enjoy a few cups of coffee." I laughed. "I love New York; don't get me wrong. There are days I miss it, but I never felt like I belonged there.'

"I get it," Gemma said. "There is something about a beach town that always feels like home. I'll let the editor know."

"Thank you." I wrapped my arms through Gemma's and pulled her toward me. "I'm really going to miss you, though."

A flashback of the day I'd first met Gemma flashed through my mind as we stared off into the ocean. I'd been fresh out of college and desperately trying to find a way to fit into the zip code that was the Upper East Side. It had been the least sketchy of all the roommate want ads I had seen. I'd sent a text and an hour later I'd been out of breath at the top of an eighth-story walk-up.

Gemma had answered on the third knock. Her hair had been blonde back then and her lips had been accentuated with a coat of bright red lipstick. I'd wondered if I'd walked into a scene from Pretty Woman, but she'd quickly put that to rest. When I had walked in, the tiny two bedroom was neat and tidy and the view of what made the city magical was right outside the living room window. All these years later and Gemma was still my go-to for everything in life.

"Something tells me you have plenty of people here to keep you company," Gemma said. "I think I see one now."

My grip dropped from Gemma's arm. I turned away from the ocean. A handsomely tan man in a pair of khaki shorts and a short sleeve white button-up was walking towards us. I had to squint through the brightness of the sun's rays, but finally I realized it was Declan.

"I thought it was you two hanging around down here," Declan said. "Too much egg cracking for you?"

I laughed. Declan seemed much more relaxed than usual. I had barely seen him since he'd left the woods with Mae in handcuffs. He had sent a text a few days later checking in on me, but that had been about it. I'd tried to think of reasons to stop by the station or text him afterwards, but nothing I'd thought of had been good enough.

"Well, hello there, detective. You're looking dapper as ever," Gemma said. "Do we have another crime to solve?"

"Haha, let's hope not for a while," he said.

"Darn. I guess it's back to crime television to get my fix. I have to say, this story will make a great podcast episode," Gemma laughed. She looked over at me and by the way she winked, I could tell I was doing a terrible job at hiding my happiness that Declan was here. "You know, I think I left my... wallet on the table in the cafe. I should probably go grab it before I give you another crime to solve. Lovely seeing you again, detective. Bye-bye."

Gemma didn't even give me a chance to react. She waved and moved quickly through the sand to the wooden stairs that led to the back patio of the cafe. Declan and I were now alone together on the beach. I clasped my hands together and pressed them against my chest, hoping it would stop the heaviness of my beating heart.

"How are you doing? Declan asked.

"Oh, I'm fine. Really." I waved my hand through the air. "I'm glad it's all over and everything is back to normal."

"Yeah. I still can't believe Wanda is gone," Declan said.

"Me neither. I also can't believe that all these years she was a fraud," I said. "It'll be interesting to see who wins the title this year. Suzy Atwater is already petitioning for the trophy all the years she was runner up."

"That doesn't surprise me."

I laughed and Declan joined in in unison. I liked the detective in Declan, but the more relaxed Declan was certainly intriguing. His face looked a little tanner and had already smiled more in the past five minutes than he had in all the time that I had spent secretly investigating with him. I liked his smile. I could've stared at it all day, but the bell rang out to signify there were five minutes left of the bake off and I knew I had to get back.

"Are you ready to go see who this year's champion is going to be?" Declan asked.

"Yeah, I'm ready. Let's go!"

I slid my flip-flops off and let my feet sink into the sand as I walked beside Declan back to the stairs. I put them on before I passed the "Shirt and Shoes Required" sign. Gemma waved to me from a table in the corner and Declan and I headed over to take a seat.

"Alright everyone, time is up!" Mayor Allen was back on the mic.

Every baker except one already had their quiche out on the table. When the last chef had pulled hers out, the eggs had oozed from the pan. Sadly, no one would be trying her quiche. Everyone else sliced a few pieces and passed them to the judges. We all waited in anticipation while each judge took a bite of the different quiches.

"Do you think they'd make it obvious if one of them was terrible?" Gemma asked.

"Oh no, it's written in the rule book. All judges have to swear to keep a smile on their face no matter what," Declan answered.

"Really?" Gemma was intrigued.

Declan couldn't hold it in any longer. A chuckle escaped from his lips. Gemma folded her arms over her chest and tried to act angry, but she too couldn't hold in the laughter. All three of us broke into a fit until Mayor Allen came back to the mic.

"And we have a unanimous decision. The winner of this year's Quiche on the Beach Bake Off is—"

I watched Suzy Atwater and the sly smile across her face. There was no doubt in her mind the name out of Mayor Allen's mouth would be hers. She slid her hands down her front to remove the wrinkles from her apron.

"Dotty Fitzgerald from Fitz's Patisserie in Bluewater!"

My jaw dropped as the room broke out into applause. Suzy's face turned bright red and she clenched her fists at her sides. When Dotty slipped past her to claim her trophy, Suzy stormed out of the room. It looked like, if the rumors were true about the French toastery, that a new rivalry had been ignited here in Blue Haven.

Once the shock had worn off, I started clapping, too. I'd had my money on Suzy, but it didn't surprise me that Dotty had what it took to win. Von Reklaw had a new review she needed to get out, after the long write-up about the shocking bake off results that is. Declan turned his chair toward me and leaned in close.

"I bet you have a little extra time on your hands since the sleuthing is over?" Declan asked.

"Well, I mean, I'm a pretty busy person—but I guess, yeah, now that having to worry about being attacked is off my to-do list, I have some more free time."

"Do you think maybe you'd want to grab dinner with me? Maybe Friday night?"

I tilted my head. Declan Grant had asked me if I wanted to have dinner with him. Of course, I wanted to have dinner with him. Not wanting to sound too eager, I counted to five in my head before answering.

"I'd like that," I said.

"Okay then. I'll pick you up at seven," he said.

"It's a date," I smiled.

Declan turned back around to watch Mayor Allen place the quiche crown on Dotty's head. I looked right over to Gemma who was silently screaming with her fists in the air. She'd been right. I was going to be okay here. Blue Haven was officially my home, now. There was plenty to keep me occupied, and first and foremost was my upcoming date with the town's most handsome detective.

THE END

ACKNOWLEDGEMENTS

There's never anyone I can thank more than you, the reader. Of all the books, you picked up mine! Thank you so much for adventuring with Veronica and all the quirky residents of Blue Haven. Your love of reading continues to let me live my dreams and I am forever grateful. For every person involved in the creation of my first cozy mystery, thank you! I'm thankful for all my writer friends, my beta readers, and my editor who make me a better writer every day.

Thank you, Mama, for being my number one fan always and spreading the word every chance you get. Thank you, dad, for reading cover to cover every book I've written. I've been blessed with the best of friends who support everything I do and cheer me on through every stage and crazy idea of my writing journey.

Shout out to my husband, who doesn't mind sleeping with the light on while I type away well after the sun goes down. Who is there to lend an ear and opinion with every question I ask while talking out loud trying to figure out what to write next. You're always in my corner. You always push me to reach my full potential and it's not lost on me how unbelievably lucky I am to have found you.

Veronica is just getting started with her life in Blue Haven! Check out the rest of this cozy mystery series:

Blueburied Waffles (Book 2)
Wrench Toast (Book 3)

ABOUT COURTNEY

Courtney is a New York native who traded in the snowy winters for the humid summers of the south and never looked back. She lives in North Carolina with her incredibly supportive and patient husband. When she's not writing, you can find her on the beach with a good book or on the search for a new coffee shop to sip an iced latte at. Sometimes, you'll also find her in front of the camera. Acting is one of her "other" side jobs in the creative life she lives. Visit www.courtneygiardina.com to read more about Courtney and her books!

Come say hi on Instagram or TikTok @courtneygfoutz

Made in the USA
Las Vegas, NV
21 February 2024

86023732R00085